Best regards

Philip E Duffy

MOMENTS

A COLLECTION OF SHORT STORIES

To order, write:
CHASE PUBLISHING
A Division of A.C.Chase Associates
23 Oak Knoll Road
Glen Rock,NJ 07452

MOMENTS

Philip Edward Duffy

CHASE PUBLISHING

MOMENTS

Cover Design by Noel Pugh

Library of Congress Catalog Card Number: 91-71199

ISBN: 0-9629651-0-3

FIRST EDITION
10 9 8 7 6 5 4 3 2 1

To my wife Natalie

CONTENTS

STRATA   1

ECHOES UNDER THE BRIDGE   15

SONATA   29

REUNION   39

UNIQUE   51

MERETRICIOUS   65

INSPIRATION   73

TEMPTATION AND SANCTITY   87

THE ALABASTER MAID   93

WANTING MORE   101

THE BEAUTY TRAP   109

THE FALSE MISS SWEENEY   125

THE CHARIOT   137

The continuum of life escapes but memory fixes upon special moments. It is by these moments that we evaluate our lives, and it is also by them that we are judged.

Philip Edward Duffy

STRATA

Mr. Ralph E. Winterton was a self-made man, his life the paradigm of the poor boy who made good. Now, a multimillionaire at the height of success, he owned a mansion in Newport, a condominium near Boothbay Harbor, and a summer house in Newfoundland.

To maintain the properties, he had gardeners, a chauffeur, two maids, and a cook. Of course, the maids related mostly to Mr. Winterton's wife, Janet. But to say that all of these possessions and servants belonged to Mr. Winterton was quite correct, since he had earned all of the money that made them possible. He was clearly the dominant person of the family and was in control of all the funds. The hiring and firing of employees was always done by Mr. R. Winterton himself, with only token consultation with his wife.

There was a simple way to get to know Mr. Ralph Winterton. All you had to do was to watch the interplay with his chauffeur, Maurice. You could hear their conversation while Mr. Winterton had his breakfast served, and invariably it was the master's voice that dominated the situation.

"I want to leave at ten, so have the car at the front door at nine-fifty sharp."

"Yes Sir, Mr. Winterton," Maurice would always

answer.

So early every morning, Maurice sat waiting in the car, motor running, for ten to twenty minutes, so that Mr. Winterton could depart as soon as he chose to appear at the door.

The conversation, one-sided, continued as they sped to work.

"Remember to pick up the items I listed, including some flowers for my wife - and keep the receipts."

"Yes Sir, Mr. Winterton."

And as they arrived at the office, Maurice would step out of the car, open the back door, and stand with his head slightly bowed. Mr. Winterton would then step forth to the sidewalk, wait for Maurice to reach for his attache case, and upon receiving it would say:

"I'll be coming out at six." This was the only signal Maurice needed to know that he should be in front of the office, well ahead of the hour of six o'clock.

Usually by the time they got home, they were both tired, and this prompted Mr. Winterton to sit in his comfortable chair and give Maurice another direction: "Fetch my newspaper, would you?" and "Why don't you start a fire in the fireplace; that would add some comfort for the evening, don't you think?"

One should not imagine that Mr. R. Winterton was totally inconsiderate of his servants. He was magnanimous when they were ill, and he gave them opportunities to travel with him. He made sure that they had a living wage and even furnished money to the older employees when they retired. But like Maurice, Mr. Ralph Winterton understood the structure of power and its relation to money. He knew the limits of his position and never demanded any services that would make his employees desperate enough to become resistant. Mr. Winterton was clearly in tune with the society in which he lived. He understood that human relationships are controlled by firmly established social strata.

As for Maurice, one would not even have suspected that he had a private life. But of course he did. To begin with, Maurice was not really Maurice. His mother had named him John McFarland. But when he came to work as a chauffeur, it was his employer's desire to have a name that matched the Rolls-Royce, and by some inexplicable logic, Mr. Winterton had elected the name, "Maurice". Of course, Maurice was born poor, and he grew up with a kind mother who struggled to survive after the early death of her husband. Before graduation from high school, Maurice was forced to quit and take a job; it was a matter of survival. He worked at odd jobs, earned very little money, made a bad marriage that ended in separation, and moved aimlessly from place to place. But he did always send a little money home to his mother. Throughout his life he had a feeling of uselessness, because he never had a sense of belonging anywhere. But in each job he took, he learned quickly and in time became a person who could serve admirably - because he could handle anything that came along. It was this ability that had pleased Mr. Winterton. He needed more than a chauffeur; he wanted an employee who could deal with anything that he required, a factotum. And Maurice had another attribute; despite his many talents he understood - and only too clearly - the social strata that controlled his position in life.

The constancy of Mr. Winterton's existence might never have been interrupted, except that he had always wanted to do something that would be viewed as adventuresome. He owned a forty foot sailboat that he had often used in the bay to entertain business associates. But no one viewed him as a real sailor, and that annoyed him.

One day, Mr. Winterton came up with a very exciting idea. He would take his boat into open ocean, sailing from Newport around the Cape and up along the coastline to Portsmouth, Portland, Boothbay Harbor, Mount Desert Island, and then to Eastport. But in order to establish himself as a "real sailor", he had an even greater adventure in mind. From Eastport, he would break out to sea, well south of Nova Scotia, and on to Sable Island. Finally, he would continue to St.John's in Newfoundland. It was an ambitious plan for an amateur and involved considerable time in open seas with no sight of land. He would take only one other person with him, and that person was a subaltern, namely Maurice. This would make it evident to all his associates that he had been the captain of the boat.

Of course, Mr. Winterton was no fool, and he recognized that he must make extensive preparations in order to carry out his idea. So he took a short course in navigation and boatsmanship in order to enlarge upon his meager experience. When Maurice heard about the undertaking, he had misgivings, but of course said nothing about it to Mr. Winterton. But he did make preparations of his own. He borrowed a book on navigation and studied it carefully; he also studied a book on sailing skills. Maurice's background in all kinds of jobs, as well as his natural aptitude in mechanics, helped him make rapid progress, which, by now, he viewed as essential to his survival. He also took personal charge of ordering all necessary supplies.

When the big week came to set sail, Mr. Winterton did it with fanfare. He invited all his friends and associates for a gala celebration to be held at his Newport mansion; a formal dinner with toasts was the order of the day. Maurice, of course, was not included, but ate with the other servants. On the final morning the guests all came down to see them off. It was a grand occasion.

Sailing out into the open ocean was, to say the least, an exhilarating experience. The ocean was a deep blue majestic calm, the bright sun was warm, and the breeze was cool. It made Mr. Winterton feel that life was worthwhile, and he sensed that, as captain, he had a new position of power. After all, he was doing what many people dream about, but never undertake - he was in the midst of a real adventure. He had made a personal commitment to go beyond the horizon in a boat under his personal control. It was not like the passive experience of all the would-be sailors who merely go on a cruise, in which, except for the view and the motion, they might as well be in any large hotel.

The first part of the trip met all the expectation that Mr. Winterton had visualized. The open ocean on one side and, successively, the Cape and those wonderful ports along the coast were exhilarating. They stopped in Portsmouth, Boothbay Harbor, and in Eastport, where Maurice was sent for supplies.

Captain Winterton felt that he was in complete

control. Still, in the next leg of the trip as the last visible land faded on the horizon, there was a creeping uncertainty, an increasing sense of the potential inadequacy of his experience and training.

As night set in and the deep blue of the water all around grew darker and darker, apprehension crept into Winterton's inner being. It was not outright fear. It was more a deepening appreciation that there was a lot of ocean out there, and that now he was facing it virtually alone.

But the night went well, and by morning Mr. Winterton was in good spirits. Everything seemed under control, and once again he was barking out orders to Maurice:

"Tighten that second starboard shroud. If this breeze continues steadily but weak, I will put out the Genoa to replace the jib."

"Yes Sir, Mr. Winterton."

Nothing much was altered in the usual form of their exchanges, except that the tone of Mr. Winterton's voice was more that of a captain than a corporate executive. The success of the sailing and Maurice's servility had the effect of reenforcing Mr. Winterton's self-assurance. On the afternoon of the second day of open sea, wafted by a gentle breeze, they looked out upon calm waters, and they were relaxed by a warm sun.

"What a beautiful sight," ventured Mr. Winterton uncharacteristically. It was partly beauty that moved him, but it was also the captain's expression of self-satisfaction that the ship, the first mate, and the large expanse of water were under his control. But it was Maurice who spoke next:

"I've never seen it quite like that. There is a deep

greenish-red forming on the horizon."

They watched as the panorama shifted. The red was now partly replaced by black spaces in that distant sky. Gradually the darker spaces began to come together; large black formations pushed away the greenish-red sky. Occasionally, a purple hue appeared amidst the other colors. In time, this mixture of colors occupied more and more of the distant sky. There was a quickening in the wind all around them, and every so often the ocean swells beneath them would lift, raising them and the boat and gently lowering them again.

It was Maurice who first expressed a dissonant voice: "I'm not sure I really like the way it looks."

Winterton was still in his captain's role and spoke accordingly: "We may get a little blow, but we can handle it."

Maurice began walking about the deck trimming the sails, tightening shackles, and checking knots.

Within about forty-five minutes, it was evident that they were in for some strong winds. The darkness had now spread over all the southern sky; the wind had reached about thirty-five knots per hour; and the boat was lurching forward, throwing a white wake to either side. Mr. Winterton and Maurice were now both obliged to work harder. Every seaman's action, which had been so easy an hour ago, now took more energy to accomplish.

The large waves, rolling in from the side, were hitting the boat, and there was a vibration athwartships with a resonance along the keelson.

At this moment something subtle was beginning to take place, something that appeared to reverse the rigid social strata that regulated the interplay between Maurice and his boss. One would hardly have noticed it, because it was a minor social incident in the midst of strenuous physical events. As one of the larger swells struck the side of the boat again, Maurice called out:

"Winterton! Head her up into the wind!" The idea made sense and was overdue - but the remarkable thing was not that. What was unusual was that Maurice had begun the sentence with the name "Winterton", not "Mr. Winterton". What was even more remarkable was that, when the command was made, Mr. Winterton heard it and simply responded by complying. There was definitely a change taking place. It was a modification, if not a reversal, of the social strata. Neither of the men had decided to make this change; it was just happening.

At first heading the boat up into the wind did steady their movement, but shortly Maurice was struggling to get the sails fully reefed. Very soon after that, all the sails had to be taken down, and only a small weather helm remained. Maurice was preparing a sea anchor, but wasn't sure if it would help or hinder.

By now they were in a full autumn storm. It had become so dark that only the white foam at the sides of the boat could be seen - the boat itself was being tossed back and forth, barely maintaining any direction. Every so often, the whole sea would light up as bolts of lightning descended to the water.

Mr. Winterton was still at the helm, but it was Maurice who had completely taken over. He barked out commands at regular intervals and, most remarkably, Mr. Winterton complied meekly. The only reason Maurice had permitted Winterton to remain at the helm was that he knew that his boss was not strong enough, or mechanically inclined enough, to handle the gear under these circumstances. What's more, he noticed that even though Winterton was at his post, he was fixed in place, almost immobile, rigidly gripping the wheel like an automaton.

As the water poured over the side and then washed away with each wave, the spray would descend over Winterton's hunched shape. As surf and wind came over his hands, they grew colder and colder against the metal of the wheel. There was nothing he could do now but to hold on tightly. He was unable to even see Maurice. Finally, as he clung desperately to his post, he became less and less aware of his surroundings. Something was happening to his sense of consciousness. And after agonizing moments of fear and cold, he began to drift into a state of semiconsciousness. He was still hanging on to the wheel - but he knew that he was slipping and that his time had come.

At this desperate moment, he felt a living body behind him. It was pressing up against him, and powerful vice-like arms surrounded him and closed upon his hands on the wheel. To Winterton it was the end, and he believed that some giant being had risen from the sea to engulf him. He was beyond fear, and he slowly relaxed his hold to allow himself to be washed away by the rushing water. But the vice-like grip from behind would not release him. In actual fact this imagined creature from the deep was Maurice, who had dragged himself along the deck, risen behind his master, and enveloped him with his body and his arms. By a superhuman effort, he had fixed his powerful hands upon the wheel and, cupping his master's body with his own, was able to prevent him from being washed away. But eventually the exertion was so great that, like a long distance runner at the end of a race, he too began to lose awareness as his body weakened. Finally, Maurice performed only in a dream-like state. During a final agony, he thought perhaps the wind was abating, but he could not be sure. In the last moments as all seemed to become more quiet, Maurice slumped around his master, but the muscles of his hands were in spasm upon the metal of the wheel. So he hung there with his master still wedged between him and the wheel. And thus they floated in a calming sea.

Strangely, it was Mr. Winterton who regained consciousness first. In the first moments of returning awareness, he thought he must be in another world, and he did not dare to move. But gradually the scene returned to him, and he once again became aware of the monstrous body behind him that clamped him to the wheel. In fear, he finally turned to face the assailant, when he realized that it was Maurice. Disengaging himself, he laid Maurice down on the deck and looked at him. He was white and rigid, and there was no movement. He must be dead. In order to take stock, Winterton stepped back to look over his surroundings. Light had returned as the storm clouds passed; the boat was listing slightly to starboard, but was riding steadily. The waves were moderate, and the boat bobbed up and down as they passed. It took Mr. Winterton some time to realize that he was really alive, but then stirrings of hope returned. He checked Maurice again, and this time he thought there was some breathing.

the next hour Winterton did nothing effective to the boat. He was still recovering, and every so often he would walk over to Maurice. At one point he noticed that Maurice was moving, and the color of his skin was returning. Eventually Maurice also regained consciousness.

The next few days were lived as if in some nebulous state. Like automatons, they began to take steps to find canned foods in the galley. Later they were able to work on bilge pumps in order to drain water from the hull. And finally, they put up a partial sail, took inexact bearings, and set a poorly determined course for the mainland, deviating from their original course for Newfoundland. To their amazement and good fortune, two days later they saw land. They moved closer to shore, where they were finally sighted and picked up by a Coast Guard cutter.

On shore, once people realized that Mr. Winterton was a man of substance, they were lodged in a luxury hotel. There was, of course, no talk about sailing back home; the boat needed extensive repairs, and, at least for now, they were through with sailing. So they telephoned home and made arrangements to take a commercial airline back.

During the flight back, their conversation avoided the whole adventure, except for a few words regarding their experience. At one point Mr. Winterton apparently felt that he had to say something. It was clear that he owed his life to Maurice, and that could not be completely ignored.

"You were great during the storm," he began. "You must have held the course at the worst point in the storm."

Maurice answered simply: "There was not much else I could do."

Mr. Winterton wanted to drop it there, but he had to say something more. "Well, you could have let me slip to the deck and preserved your strength to save yourself."

Maurice hesitated a moment, and then he said: "I really couldn't do that to anybody, Mr. Winterton."

And that was it for their discussion. When they landed in Newport, Janet Winterton was at the airport with many of their friends. The whole episode was being viewed as a great adventure, and their friends were there to celebrate. Mr. Winterton was quickly swept up by the group, but he looked back before he walked with them toward the airport restaurant. He looked back toward Maurice, and he called out:

"Will you pick up the bags?"

When they reached the restaurant, they ordered some bottles of wine. Maurice showed up a little later, and he sat with the bags in the lobby. At one point Mr. Winterton came by and said: "Why don't you get yourself something to eat and tell them to just put it on my tab."

After the meal, Janet Winterton gave Maurice the car keys and told him where to get the car. Soon he was back with the long limousine, and they all climbed in. Maurice drove.

When they got home, Mr. Winterton and Janet Winterton retired to the living room. Maurice joined the cook and the gardeners, who wanted to hear all about the trip. At one point Mr. Winterton came by and said that he and his wife needed to have a fire in the fireplace. He asked one of the gardeners to do it, saying that Maurice was entitled to a little rest. He told them that Maurice had been a great sailor.

In the parlor Janet Winterton made an observation to Mr. Winterton: "I'm not sure what is happening to Maurice, but he seems a little different. He used to be in the right place at the right time, right away. Now I had to call on him several times in order to remind him to do things which I used to take for granted." Winterton took a moment to absorb that, and then he responded casually: "It may take him a while to get back into the swing of things, but I'm sure he'll be all right."

After a week, Mr. Winterton was ready to go back to work. He dropped by the kitchen to tell Maurice to have the car ready; he wanted it at the usual time, promptly.

"Yes Sir, Mr. Winterton," came the regular answer.

Afterwards, Mr. Winterton made his ritualistic second command: "And don't forget to get the newspaper." Then he did feel obliged to add something less formal. "Feels good to get back into the old routine, doesn't it?"

Maurice hesitated; he was holding back, and deliberately considering his answer. But then he answered simply: "Yes Sir, Mr. Winterton, I'm sure it is."

ECHOES UNDER THE BRIDGE

After the death of his wife, George Brennan, who had just turned sixty-five, decided to retire and find a new house. He was a man of modest means, so his choice of houses was limited, but he found one down by the river where he was sure he could find a new life - with peace and quiet. Where the river crossed the town it was really more like a canal, with cement walls on either side and a path going along beside it. An old bridge crossed the canal; it was one of those old bridges made of large stone blocks arranged in the form of an arch. The path that went along the canal passed beneath the bridge. The scene was not the most beautiful in the world, but for George Brennan, with his limited income, it was special. And it met one of his requirements; it allowed him to "get away from it all". The seclusion near the canal and bridge furnished what he needed. The home itself was a simple brown frame house, built in the early nineteen-forties. It had one great redeeming feature; there was a large screened-in porch facing out toward the canal. The house was built on a slope, so that from the porch one could see the canal and the bridge below. There was no doubt about why George Brennan had bought the house. He knew he would sit there and enjoy the water going by, as well as the quiet.

Since the death of his wife, George Brennan had been much afraid of loneliness. He knew that he needed a house that would not "close him in" but would instead present a connection to the outside world. Soon he was on his porch every evening. And it was not long before he congratulated himself on his house purchase. Not only did he have quiet on his porch, but it was a "window" to other people. Every evening he could see them walk on the path which wound along beside the canal - then they would pass under the bridge. Often they sat for a time on a bench which was located near the canal just before the bridge. And so George Brennan had solitude, but he also had the mild entertainment that older people enjoy at seeing others going by.

The distance from the house to the canal was such that George could see the people very closely, but it was a bit far to hear what they were saying. He found it entertaining to sit there and speculate upon whom they might be and what they were saying to each other. Soon he discovered a most remarkable thing. As people passed beneath the bridge, there was a resonance of their voices from the stone of the underside of the bridge. It created an echo that enhanced the sound and carried clearly enough for George to understand part of what they were saying. So, every evening George sat on his porch where he could not be seen. As people sat on the bench, he would try to guess from their appearance and behavior what was taking place in their lives. A moment later when they passed beneath the bridge, he would hear snatches of their conversation - often enough to confirm or reject his speculations.

Early one evening George saw a middle-aged couple

walking along the canal. They stopped and sat on the bench. George remembered that he had seen them upon several occasions before. The man was very obviously decisive in personality - she was clearly sweet and demure. But this time they were different. The man was talking more actively, as if he were explaining something to her. She sat quietly keeping her hands folded in her lap. George noticed what an attractive woman she was - not glamorous, but comely, with a thin face and a well proportioned body. There was a look on her face at this moment that George recognized in women; it was that tentative look, that "holding back" expression. George had learned, from experience with his wife, that whenever she looked like that he had to remain most careful about what he said. So, George concluded that she was very displeased but had not yet stated her position. The man, on the other hand, was doing a lot of explaining, perhaps too much. George wondered if he himself was right in his surmise about them; or could it be something different? Was she only sad? But no, it was definitely "that look".

By now George was very curious. Would he ever know the answer? It all depended upon what they did next. It was amazing how much George could surmise from their expressions and their posture. But was he right?

The woman stood up. The man followed suit. Which way would they go? " Ah, good," George said to himself, "she's moving toward the bridge." Sure enough, from below the bridge George heard just enough to divine the answer.

The echoes of the man's voice came through first.

"I tell you it's all in the past. She does not mean

anything to me now." There was a long pause, and George was afraid he might never know her reaction. But then it came, slowly but decisively:

"You don't understand. I'm doing my best to decide whether you mean anything to me."

They came back from under the bridge, walking slowly and without talking. They continued along the canal. The issue was clearly hanging in the balance.

It was several months before George saw this couple again. He had begun to believe that they had broken up and moved away. But finally one evening they appeared again.

They looked very much as before, but there were subtle changes in their comportment. They did not stroll in their previous manner. Their walk was a little faster and more business-like. And when they came to the bench, they walked right passed it. George thought he would probably never know her decision; however when they passed under the bridge a few sentences seemed to say it all. It was her voice that came through:

"No," she said categorically, "we don't want to go to the shore this year; the children and I are going to Maine for the summer. There is no reason why you can't come up on weekends. We can visit with your parents in the fall when they drive through."

So it was settled! She was apparently staying with him. But the demure little wife was no more. George made a final evaluation as the couple walked away. That man may have convinced her to stay with him, and his philandering may have been exciting, but it had exacted a price, a heavy one.

After this episode, George Brenner realized what a fortuitous purchase the house and well situated porch had been. For a man adjusting to living alone, this seemed like a special treatment program. He always had company, and he could try to know the people who walked past by their behavior. Often he could confirm or reject his theories according to the words that came from under the bridge. There was, of course, an issue of propriety. Should he sit there unperceived by the people he was surveying? It was, without any question, peeping and eavesdropping at the same time. But George justified himself without effort. He was, after all, just sitting on his own porch and had not planned to snoop.

His next visitors were two women. One was old enough to be the mother of the younger one, yet they chatted as if they were just friends. This was a puzzle for George. The pair came by many times, but their attitude was consistently the same, and George made no headway in understanding their relationship. At times they sat on the bench. Both were well dressed, neatly but not expensively. The puzzling thing was that they did look a little bit alike; however, they definitely did not act like relatives.

One day as they sat on the bench, it was evident that there was some new tension between them. The older woman took the younger woman's hand; but the young one nervously withdrew it. Then suddenly, they both exploded into tears and hugged each other. But after that the younger woman drew back, as if she were unsure whether she wanted to allow this intimate emotional expression. Unfortunately for George, the episode ended when they suddenly stood up and walked away without passing under the bridge.

Several weeks went by. George could only wonder at all the possible interpretations. Finally one evening he saw them again. They were very friendly now, holding hands. Speculations raced by in George's mind. Later, he had to admit to himself that the one true answer never went through his mind.

This time the two women walked slowly under the bridge, and he heard a voice, clearly the younger one, saying:

"I could hardly believe it."

The response was measured: "I know it must have been a terrible shock to you." Then, several more things were said, but George could not hear quite well enough to understand. He was about to concede that he would never obtain an answer, but then an echo came through from under the bridge, and he was able to hear a part of a sentence:

"I had given up all hope of ever finding my ....", and then the words sounded like "meal other". After that the pair departed. George was left there, "hanging". He felt frustrated. How could they do that to him? People should speak more clearly. But then, George knew that that was a ridiculous thing to say or think. So he put it out of his mind and then settled down to a late supper. All through his meal, the puzzle came back to him. He could not completely forget about it, and it began to make him nervous. Finally, he decided he had to put it out of his mind, and he began to watch television. But, at intermissions and during the ads, the question popped back into his mind. He became annoyed and said to himself, "enough", and once again he put it out of his mind.

At eleven o'clock George went to bed. His eyes closed, and slowly he became less and less aware of his surroundings. He was slowly falling asleep. He began to dream and, of course, it was the two women who were part of it. He saw them under the bridge, and he dreamed he heard their last sentence again and again, with those last two words that sounded like "meal other". In his sleep George became extremely agitated, and he suddenly awakened out of his dream. As he did so, he heard himself exclaim out loud:

"The words were not 'meal other'; they were 'real mother'." And so, he was now perfectly sure; the sentence had been, "I had given up all hope of finding my real mother." George could now breath a big sigh of relief, and he fell into a deep and restful sleep.

For a time after that, George saw only some of his "regular customers", as he called them. But late one evening, two little boys showed up. They were about ten years old, reasonably well kept, but not from wealthy families. They were very agitated and clutching something that they passed back and forth between them. It looked like a large envelope. When the boys saw the bench, they rushed over to it, looked around to see if anyone was watching, and began to open the envelope. What they pulled from the envelope was money, lots and lots of bills. George could not see the denominations of the bills, but even if they were one dollar bills, there was quite a stack of them.

Now George had a dilemma. If this was a theft, shouldn't he report it? And yet, he could not make an accusation without knowing how they had obtained this envelope. Nor could he really walk up to them and ask - they would probably run away.   Also, it was always possible that they had earned it and saved it, however unlikely that seemed. So George was forced into his usual pattern.   He only sat quietly and watched.

The boys began to count the money meticulously. As they finished, one of the boys held both hands up to his head, while the other one threw his arms up into the air. The sum was big!

Next, they began to divide the money. Finally one placed his share into the envelope, and the other one stuffed his wad into his pocket. They walked away under the bridge. Their animated conversation came clearly through. It was what might be called a little boys' moral discussion. One warned that when you found money, you had to return it. The other one believed that "finders are keepers". Then one became concerned that the money had come from a mobster; it was even a possibility that those gangsters might come after them.   Finally there was a discussion about telling their parents, a consideration that was very quickly ruled out.

George realized that he had never before heard a conversation so clearly or fully.   Probably the boys' excitement caused their high-pitched and penetrating voices to carry further.   In the end they walked away with their loot. In succeeding days George watched the papers for any report of robbery - or lost money - but there was none. George realized that a complete answer to this story would never come; the boys would certainly not be back with the money.   But at least George believed that he had part of the answer; there was no question that the money had been found - not earned.

After that there was a prolonged period with no visitors; but a time came when George had an experience he would never quite recover from. He sat one evening on his porch after dark. He could not see the edge of the canal, the bench, or the bridge. He was about to go in when he heard sounds from under the bridge. So he listened.

The voices were from two men. They were guttural, and George could not discriminate the words. They spoke in deep, short accents. The voices were low but threatening. And then it happened! There were terrible, but muffled, sounds. There was a thud and then a moan. But after that the voices stopped, and then it all became very quiet.

This was the first time that George ceased to enjoy his secret observation post. He was excited by what he had heard, but he felt uncomfortable. Something ominous was going on, and he was a partial witness to it. He thought of notifying the police, but was too afraid. So, he sat for over an hour trying to hear any further sound. But nothing more was heard, and he never saw anyone leaving. Finally George gave up and went to bed, but he had a restless night. The threat had been very real and very close. He was a part of it, and yet he wasn't.

Later, George's worst fears became reality when the newspaper announced that a murder had taken place. The body was found in the water near the old canal, floating face up. There was evidence of a blow on the man's skull, the result of a blunt object. Again, George's sense of duty made him want to report all that he had heard. But what good would it do? There would be no information useful to the police, and it would identify him as a witness. Retribution was possible. George remained silent.

But this time, George could not completely put the event out of his mind. And his own complicity, at least moral, would give him no rest. The situation was so bad for George, personally, that he decided he had to do something to separate himself from it. Finally, he decided that he must move away from this house!

He called a real estate agent, and all necessary preparations were made. The agent thought it best to put off advertising for at least three weeks, because sales would pick up then, and the newspaper ads would be more productive.

So during the next three weeks George continued to use his porch, but he was uncomfortable. A deeply oppressive preoccupation was with him day and night - it was the knowledge of murder having occurred so close. Then too, he had heard it happen! So the porch had little pleasure for him now, and George waited eagerly for the advertisement of his house, and even better, the possible sale of it.

But events surrounding the canal would not wait for George's schedule. As it happened, there were two more events that took place during the next few weeks.

The first event began when he saw a young man and his girl friend approach the bench. They sat and talked. At first they appeared to be bantering with one another. Then, they turned serious, looking deeply into each other's faces. He was sliding one hand over hers as it rested on the bench. After a while they sauntered hand in hand under the bridge. George heard the young man's voice:

"I don't know if I'm saying this right," he began, "but I know I've always loved you, and I don't know what I would do if you refused to be my wife."

She came back at him a little coquettishly - she could afford to, since it was he who had taken the plunge and made himself vulnerable to refusal. She was safe. So she answered with a question:

"You're a little round-about, you know. Are you asking me to marry you?"

"I guess I am."

"You've got to stop guessing and say it, John."

"All right. I'm asking you, and please don't say no."

George could not hear all her answer, but there was a yes, and then again a yes with a little slur that must have been melodious for his ears. And then the answer came even more clearly as they emerged from under the bridge, arm in arm and kissing all the way. So George went to bed feeling better that night.

And the very next week he witnessed an old couple walking along the canal. They were clearly retired, but they too were holding hands. She had a corsage pinned to her dress. He was in a suit, definitely his best. They both looked well but very old. They rested for a long time on the bench. Things moved slowly at this age. And they savored every minute of this day. There was no excitement, but they were comfortable, happy, trusting, and yes, loving. From beneath the bridge George heard only one sentence by the man:

"I still feel very young, and I can't believe it's been fifty-eight years today."

It was the way George had felt - in those last years with his wife. Long after the couple had left, George sat on his porch and dreamed of the good days that he remembered.

A week later the real estate man showed up one morning, full of energy and ready to move. "The ad is in the paper, and we should get some action soon."

George looked at the agent as if he had taken an uncalled for action. "I'm sorry, but I've decided to stay."

That was a shocking surprise for the eager agent, and he made remonstrances:

"I don't understand you. You were very definite the last time I saw you. Did something happen, or what?" George was a bit embarrassed, but he knew exactly what he wanted now, so he was not about to change his course. He chose his words with care and spoke slowly:

"You see, something did happen a few weeks ago that made me want to leave. But then more things took place, and I thought back upon my life and everything I had experienced - sitting right here on this porch. And finally I decided that I like it."

The real estate man had absolutely no idea what this client was talking about, but he could see that George would not change his mind again, so he stopped complaining. But he was still curious: "I don't understand exactly what it is that one could experience on a porch that would make you change your mind like that."

George was not about to recount his secret life, but he decided to give a general answer:

"I've seen and heard some terrible things from here, but I've also seen wonderful things. Now, I've decided that none of it was different from life in general. I've lived long enough to know that you can avoid only a few of life's experiences; beyond that you have to accept."

So George stayed - and he looked, and he listened. And often he thought he should write it all down. But he never did; he just lived with it and enjoyed the parts that were good.

By and by, he even met the visitors to the canal. He sauntered down casually and chatted with some of them, and even helped a few who were in trouble. George was never alone any more.

About two years later, the real estate man came by, just to see if George had changed his mind.

"No," George said, "I've been very happy here."

"Well I can see that," said the agent. "There is a nice view from the porch."

George answered thoughtfully: "It's much more than that. There's been a whole new life for me here. And you see, I like the echoes under the bridge."

SONATA

He saw her first at a private concert in one of those plush rooms in which the solid walls were made of oak, its rich grain showing darkly through the varnish that glowed from repeated waxing. There were barely more than sixty carefully selected people attending, all in deep comfortable upholstered chairs resting on thick carpeting. The lights were low, and they were reflected only softly from the polished wood.

He remembered how he came to be there. His sense of values, as yet poorly developed, would never have motivated him to spend a whole evening at a private concert. But his professor of music had distributed extra tickets, so the desire to impress him was mixed with the advantage of free admission.

Now he sat after dining out - and a few good glasses of wine. He was ensconced in one of those deep comfortable chairs, surrounded on all sides by equally comfortable-looking people. There was an air of dignity and wealth, combined in people and surroundings. He felt satisfied. He could last through the evening in a restful dormant state. He was not prepared for what happened next.

From the back of the room she wafted in and down the aisle. She seemed to flow along with the evening gown all white, its trailing hem brushing lightly along the carpeted surface. He was aware that this electrifying presence had just transformed the room as she moved effortlessly toward the piano at the front. There could be no doubt about it, the performer had arrived; and she had in an instant turned every eye toward her without as yet having produced a single sound from the instrument.

The concert selections included Vivaldi and Bach, and then the Beethoven Sonata Number 23 in F minor. Listening, at first casually, but later intently, he experienced a transition as the realization came to him that music meant more to him than he had known. For the first time, not just the melody, but the structure of music took on a beauty of its own. And those lessons at the piano, which he had been forced to take some years ago, now re-engaged his attention with new meaning. His young mind, now somewhat more mature than before, could hear and see those meaningless chidlhood lessons in a new light.

To say that the passion that stirred within him was all derived from the music would not reflect the whole experience, for now his eyes were fixed upon the shape of this woman at the piano. Her dark beauty, the long hair, and the slim legs that worked the pedals all served to rivet his attention toward her and the sound. Introspective as he was, he wondered if it was mostly the woman, and not the music, that made his perception more sensitive than in former days. Still, if she had played badly, he knew she would not have generated what he felt now. And if technically she had without fault moved through the difficult passages, but lacked the feeling and the interpretive sense he craved, she could not have affected him as she did. So it was she who moved him, but it was also the composer's pen.

He watched the flowing movements of her arms with their effortless grace, transmitting to the hall the andante of a distant composer. In more animated passages the quickening pace and much greater effort brought a pink hue to the white skin, and her more rapid breathing came with visible excitement and parting of her lips. He felt, at one point, that she looked directly at him.   His own breathing was faster now, and there was moisture in his hands; he knew that he had never before been moved so strongly by music.

The performance over, she flowed past him up the aisle, and he searched her face to share the new sensation; but now the face was impervious, herself untouchable, and only a scent of perfume remained after her.

Slowly rising from his chair, he started to leave, but suddenly an authoritative and familiar voice interrupted:

"Johnston, I'm pleased to see that you came."

It was his professor: "I hope you noted the variations in the Sonata form which we discussed in class. There were some weaknesses in the interpretation of the first movement, but overall it was a very creditable performance."

"I thought it was too," Johnston ventured.

He had not noticed any weakness in the first movement, but he knew that professors always said something negative when they appraised anything. The professor was now greeting other guests, but turned back briefly to Johnston:

"There's a reception upstairs; you should be there

and meet the soloist."

To meet her seemed too much for Johnston. She was now an ideal that embodied everything he had ever wanted in a woman. And in a brief interlude she had opened for him a new realization of what sound could be, of what it could mean to him.

After a discreet interval, he did proceed to the party in honor of the pianist. There was a reception line. As he shook her hand her eyes were expressionless, but he thought she held his hand longer than expected. He told her that the audience was very much indebted to her for the performance - and then he moved on. Several glasses of wine later, they stood next to each other again by chance, and they spoke once more.

The progression of events during the next hour appeared incredible to Johnston. From hesitant initial responses, they seemed to drift together repeatedly. But Johnston knew, at least in part, what made her irresistible to him. Never before had he experienced physical attraction so strong to a woman who also brought forth from him new intellectual and artistic appreciation. The combination was more than he had ever hoped to find in a single person.

An obsession quickly overwhelmed him; to have her, to possess her, would be unlike any ordinary physical pleasure. It seemed impossible that a rapidly moving need in her as well could bring them toward each other so precipitously. But as most of the audience left, a few of her friends were invited to continue the celebration at her apartment. And through a chance connection of a friend of hers, who also knew Johnston, he was invited as well. So later that very night, he came to her apartment. There were about twenty people there, and the goodness of the wine made the late night hours pass quickly to reach that time when guests began to leave.

It was at this moment that she did something that Johnston could hardly have hoped for. She stood before him with a glass of wine and leaned slightly closer to him saying:

"I hope you won't have to leave yet. I need more time to unwind."

And so, as each guest in turn retired, Johnston delayed. It was he, the stranger, who lasted until the end. And finally, these two young people, full of wine and exhilaration, were left alone.

Many years later he would recall the rest of that night mostly as feelings. He remembered her expressionless face but yielding body as he pulled her gently to him. He remembered also the warm lips and now impassioned movements of her body, with faster breathing and a pink color upon her white skin, and with the rising excitement a frenzied grasping for the experience that would remain unmatched.

In the weeks and months that followed, they did not see each other. It was as if they both knew that the uncontrolled impulse that had driven them together would be difficult to regain.

But Johnston was unrequited; he had come close to an ideal. Day after day the desire for the sensation he had felt, during and after that concert, returned. He realized that he could not achieve his goal by simply relating to her as he might with any ordinary human being. He dreaded the possibility of being with her once again but feeling disappointment, if she were now like any other girl he had ever met. So he determined to search for his ideal by looking for her again at one of her recitals, in the same setting in which he had come close to reaching an ultimate experience.

So on a Saturday night, Johnston came again to one of her performances. To say that he was there only to try to recapture a simple entertainment would be to grossly understate it. He was by now obsessed with a single thought, even more a single need, to feel once again that sensation that he had felt on that first night when he heard her play.

This time, he sat in the very first row. She would enter from the back of the room, down the aisle, and would have to pass directly in front of him, and very close. Would she give a sign of recognition? Would she even pause, or smile? Anticipation mounted.

When she came, her entrance was very much as it had been the first time. A sudden flowing apparition which glided down the aisle, accompanied by that same rustling of the evening dress, this time red. In an instant she passed before him. Almost expressionless, she stepped lightly, looking toward the piano ahead. There was a suggestion of a smile on her face, but not directed at Johnston specifically. Rather, she had a mysterious quality which was being shared with the whole audience. But Johnston's state was such that, when a corner of her gown touched his foot, he felt certain that it was an intentional communication meant just for him. Her perfume remained in the air, and Johnston breathed it in, slowly and deeply.

Like a partial anesthesia, it seemed to envelop him, and he saw her as if in an excited but dream-like state.

She was now seated at the piano, and her position was such that Johnston faced her nearly directly. Above the piano he could see her face and shoulders, the upper part of her breasts, and a little of the gown. Below, he saw her feet and a part of her legs as they reached for the pedals.

Her recital was flawless. She played Brahms and Chopin. But mostly it was the last piece she played that moved him; it was once again Beethoven's Sonata Number 23 in F Minor. It was unusual to play these pieces in that order, but then nothing about her was conventional. And that Sonata reverberated over and over within his inner hearing. Clearly the passion that he felt was emanating in large part from the music itself, but at the same time he saw again her white skin, and the parting of her lips; he felt once more her impassioned movements, much as he had when he had been with her through the night. But most of all, that obsession for complete fulfillment was his at this moment, as never before. He felt that he had briefly attained an ideal, an ideal that had taken hold of his very soul; but he could not name it, he could not hold it, and he could not recreate it at will.

It was not entirely the woman or the sound that he wanted. There was something else. Try as he would, he could not understand what more he could want. And yet he knew that he was searching for an unidentified desire. During the weeks that followed, this haunting need for something he could not name was with him constantly, and for months after that he kept brooding over what now seemed like an unidentified assailant. Melded into this inner turmoil were the woman and that Sonata she had played so well.

And then it came; it was a sharp turn in his life during the next year. Like a deluge, he found himself more and more involved in music. And finally he became so engrossed with it, that he enrolled in a graduate program for the performing arts. So now his life took shape, and in time it was he who became the performer. Eventually he was launched into that grueling career, which concert pianists live for, but must also endure. And the next thirty years of his life moved so fast that they rushed past him year after year.

And now, as an old man, Johnston sat before his living room window, looking out to the trees and the lake below. The panes of glass were hazy before his eyes, and his eyelids drooped slightly, but he remembered still. He wondered why he had never tried to see her again. But now he did understand, at least in part, what had happened to him during and after her concerts. It had been a search for his own identity. Now so many years later, he could recall hundreds of concerts, after which the critics either praised or criticized his interpretation. He wondered if in all that time, he had ever experienced a feeling as intense or complete as he had during her first concert, and after. Love and youth had melded then with a discovery of his life's work. Music had been enveloped in his first love, and the power of its feelings was in the freshness of it.

He could look back now upon his career with satisfaction. He had no regrets. But to take the two most intense experiences of his life, and to fuse them into a marvelous obsession, was something he had been granted but once.   And now the strongest experience he could recover was in the memories of times past, in those images of young beauty and sounds, when first they stirred within his soul.

REUNION

The letter came hidden in the stack of advertisements. Frank and Irene Dunham paid little attention. But in the evening, as they were relaxing in the den, Irene showed it to Frank.

"It's our thirtieth high school reunion. We should go!"

Frank merely shrugged his shoulders:

"I simply cannot imagine what one gets out of those things. Everybody looks terrible, and worse than that, when they look at you, it's easy to see in their expression that you look just as bad to them. On top of that there are reports of some who died, many more who are now sick, and other depressing stories."

Irene was not so easily put off. "You have always looked on the dark side. At a thirtieth reunion, enough time has gone by so that it is interesting to see what everyone did with his or her life."

Frank persisted, "You're not going to get me there, but you can go if you like."

It probably would have been dropped right there, except that Frank met one of his classmates in the barber shop. They both laughed at the way their wives were so completely fascinated by the reunion, while they both knew that it would be an absolute bore. But after a while,

Frank's classmate, Roger Foley, brought up an interesting question:

"Do you remember Isabel?"

"Do I remember Isabel?   I guess no one forgets Isabel!   That girl had more boys on the string than anyone I've ever known."

"You're right, Frank.   She was, without any question, the most alluring girl in the class."

"I'll go you one better," said Frank.   "In all my life since then, I've never seen a woman whose every movement expressed such sensuality.   Remember those long legs and the flowing of the clinging skirts she wore.   That woman reached out to men without saying anything."

Roger concurred, and the barber laughed.   He remembered Isabel too.

That night Frank was dining with his wife and surprised her.   "If you're really set on going to the reunion, I guess it would not hurt me to go."

Not long after that Irene was having lunch in a nice little restaurant with Roger Foley's wife, Jennifer, and learned that she and her husband were going to the reunion too.

"You know what it is?" ventured Jennifer.   "The boys have got the idea that Isabel will be there, and they want to see her."

That did not disturb either of the wives, and Irene said it best: "Boy, are they going to be disappointed! She's about forty-seven or more by now, and they won't even recognize her."   They both laughed.   They laughed even more after Dorothy Hingham joined them at the table, told them she and her husband, Fred, were also going, and that Fred was eager to go because he wanted to see Isabel. That sent them into hysterics, and the luncheon ended up being one of those times when people begin to laugh at anything that anyone says.

The reunion idea, which had begun casually for all of them, became more and more exciting because of the anticipation created by the mere mention of Isabel! The husbands couldn't wait to be with her, and the wives were wildly entertained by the thought of their spouses' certain discomfiture. When the great night finally came there were lots of phone calls criss-crossing between Irene and Jennifer, and from Dorothy to Irene, and Jennifer to Dorothy. The last call was by Irene to Jennifer:

"You wouldn't believe what this husband of mine is going through to get dressed! In the last thirty years I haven't seen him like that. All afternoon he's been fussing about the shape of the tuxedo and whether he should or should not wear a boutonniere. The cummerbund could hardly stretch around him - and he had to keep loosening his belt. It's really a riot!"

"I know, I know," responded Jennifer. "Roger has been doing the same thing. I bet their mothers were the last to see them go through those gyrations before the Junior Prom, which was more than thirty years ago. I tell you Irene, this has got to be the funniest thing I've ever seen in my life. They don't even know how funny they look."

When the three couples were ready, they all met in order to drive in one car. There were many knowing glances between the ladies; as for the men, they were wildly exhilarated!

Upon entering the hotel ballroom, it was evident that Isabel had not arrived. Forty-five minutes later almost everyone was there, but no Isabel. The wives said they wanted to go freshen up, but actually they wanted to talk.

"Nine to one she doesn't even show up," was Dorothy's first remark. That did it! The other ladies could hardly contain themselves, and soon they were all giggling uncontrollably. When they returned to the ballroom, they were barely able to manage a calm and serious appearance. The men were edgy.

Suddenly there was a hush in the room. It was apparent that there were other men who were anxious about Isabel's arrival, and now a rumor was spreading that she was in the lobby. Many men were nonchalantly glancing toward the door. Finally it opened, and there she was!

Isabel stood there resplendent. It was as if time had passed her by. She was certainly more mature, but her beauty was untouched. The long slim legs, the trim waist, the full bosom, and the model's face were all there. Her body and the outlines of her high cheek bones showed no signs of any increase in weight. The enticing eyelashes were slick with mascara, and the rouge was delicately applied to her cheeks. And when she moved, the same languid sensuality was fully there, and every gesture was an invitation.

For a moment she paused near the entrance, obviously enjoying the effect that she was having on the whole hushed congregation. Her power over the assembled guests was even greater than it had been in high school. Clearly, only she remained as before, seemingly untouched by age.   And this was guilelessly made evident and expressed by her, in her usual charmingly seductive way.

The wives were not laughing now. In fact nothing seemed funny now. They attempted light conversation - all the time looking away from Isabel. But it was to no avail. Shocked beyond every expectation, they tried their best to continue as if nothing had happened.

But soon Isabel began her old pattern, circulating from man to man. Was she married?   Apparently not. It was whispered from mouth to mouth that she had been, briefly, but that she soon returned to living freely by herself. But this was only a manner of speaking. She was by herself only when she chose.

Irene, Jennifer, and Dorothy all experienced a glimmer of hope as someone pointedly questioned whether Isabel had done anything worthwhile in her life.   They assumed that she had frittered it away.   But as it turned out, they were overwhelmingly wrong on that count as well. Isabel had indeed done a great deal. She had built up a dress-making shop into a large business, trading in women's dresses in Europe, Scandinavia, and the United States. One would not want to say that all the ladies at the reunion were trying to find fault with Isabel - but no matter what they did, they could not fault her. Isabel continued circulating amongst the crowd.   When meeting other women she had a most genial greeting; it was even difficult for them to dislike her, although many succeeded. It was really only her extreme beauty and her expensive gown, with an aura of wealth and success, that aroused their innate jealousy. But in any objective evaluation, she was faultless. The other women could only wince as they watched the husbands taking turns offering her drinks and enticing her to dance. And it was the dancing that the wives could not stand. Isabel had a way of pressing her body against the man and then following his every movement, as if she were a part of him.

At about eleven o'clock Jennifer suggested that she had a busy day coming up, and perhaps they should go home soon. There was immediate agreement from Irene and Dorothy. Frank, Fred, and Roger could hardly be reached in order to start this idea on its way. They were very busy and showing no signs of tiring. So for about an hour and a half, there were reminders to leave and rejoinders to stay. Finally the wives became more demanding, and the group slowly gathered to leave.

In the car, Fred suggested that they must organize more reunions. Frank and Roger decided that there was no reason why they should not plan to invite some of the class to their homes. The women talked about other things, but actually, they spoke very little. When they all reached their own houses their patterns varied. Jennifer had a short argument with her husband about hanging up his coat properly; Dorothy was asleep even before Fred came to bed; and Irene stayed awake thinking.

Despite the men's plans to the contrary, a home reunion never materialized. But the ladies went on diets, and the barber shop conversations were more lively. It was there that Frank brought up a special subject when he met Fred on a Saturday afternoon:

"That was some reunion! And wasn't she really something?"

He didn't even specify who the "she" was, but Fred

answered as if he had: "I could hardly believe my eyes. We could almost have stepped out of the school thirty years ago and back in the next day, and she wouldn't have looked any different. A few people are like that; they get even better looking with time. But it's a rare thing."

The barber joined in; he wanted to hear all about Isabel. So the men talked and talked, and then they laughed about the good old days and about their exploits with Isabel.

The rest of that year was uneventful. The three couples were back in their daily routine, but the reunion had created lingering tensions. Now, when Irene, Jennifer, and Dorothy met for lunch, they no longer laughed about the reunion. The memories were unpleasant for them, and they were unable to accept with grace that Isabel, of all people, should have had a successful career - and on top of that had managed to remain slim and beautiful.

At home, they all had persisting, minor, but irritating marital difficulties about the reunion. None of them were about to break up over it, but somehow things were not quite the same. The men were living with a startling illusion, a beautiful illusion, that somehow it was possible to remain forever young and beautiful. The wives were living with the harsher discovery that for some people, or at least for one person, that apparent illusion was a reality. The result was not too good. It was not so much that any of these couples were less devoted to each other, but all had become irritable. It seemed to affect their daily capacity to be at peace with each other, and with themselves. The husbands now believed that something may have passed them by during their lives, and the wives felt insecure.

Frank kept talking with Roger about that possible get-together at home with classmates which they had proposed; but try as they might, there was no support for it and no invitation.

Two years later, there was some talk about another reunion. It started off with enthusiasm, but then they heard that Isabel would be in Paris to look over the latest fashions. The reunion committee decided that it was really too soon after such a big party two years before. During the third and the fourth years there was much speculation, but no action. The ladies were not keen about it.

But after the fifth year everything seemed to come together again. The reunion committee was now composed of six men and two women, and they had voted for another big one.

The men started the whole pattern of anticipation all over again, and the wives were on their diets again. For Frank, Roger, and Fred, it even replaced talk about baseball. The wives called each other just as they had before the last reunion, but the conversations were not the same; they were guarded and without humor.

The big night came along soon enough. And just as before the three couples went together. In the hotel ballroom the crowd was very much like last time - a little older of course, but not perceptibly so. Isabel had not arrived! Jennifer waited until a time when the husbands were busy talking with each other, and then she commented to Dorothy and Irene:

"Same old pattern! She's holding off until the last

minute. That grand entrance again!"

There was an even more prolonged wait than last time. But finally the main door swung open and Isabel appeared. There was a sudden quiet in the room as people caught their breath. Isabel was completely changed!

Her face was pale and drawn. The muscles of her legs looked flabby. Her shoulders were drooping, and she was bent forward at the neck. She walked stiffly and with much difficulty, apparently forcing herself to make a great effort to bring her legs forward. Even her hair had turned a little gray. In short, there was a complete trans-figuration.

With a sober look, Frank made his way over to greet her. She was as pleasant as ever, but her voice was weak. Finally, Frank had to ask the question: "Is everything all right, Isabel?"

She answered just as forthrightly as ever:

"Well, not really. You see, I've been sick this year. There was an operation. And I have osteoporosis which resulted in what they called a pathological fracture of one of the bones in my spinal column. That's what makes me stooped over."

There was little else to be said. Age, and its assembled host of ailments, had now caught up with Isabel as well.

The ride home was quiet. The men, of course, were downcast. It was not just the young Isabel who was gone, it was also a warm illusion, full of youth and vigor and beauty.

As for the women, their reaction was even more fascinating. For the moment, they didn't say much either.

But a few days later, they got together for lunch in that favorite restaurant. First, they talked about other things, but then Irene brought it up and asked a question:

"I think I need an honest answer from myself and from you. Were you both a little jealous of Isabel after the first reunion?" Jennifer answered: "If you had asked me that before the second reunion, I think I would have denied it. But when I saw how Isabel had changed, I came to realize that if it could happen to her, it would happen to all of us. And then I felt more sorry than jealous."

For a moment none of them spoke. Then Dorothy followed up:

"I knew the boys were kidding themselves - I mean before the first reunion. But I never realized that I was fooling myself too. Somehow this time when I saw Isabel like that, it came to me that I always pretended that age was not catching up to me. And when I saw Isabel, I was suddenly older."

And finally it was Irene who summed it up:

"This morning I was thinking of our husbands and ourselves. Do you know what I wished? I wished I could be jealous again, and they all could be funny again."

There still was one more comment about it all, and it came from Jennifer:

"This reunion business wasn't all bad. Do you know that Roger and I are now spending more time together than we ever did? He even held my hand the other day."

At home, Frank Dunham sat in his den with a book in his hands, although he was really thinking about his wife, Irene. He was thinking about how much he loved her and needed her. But in the background he was playing a record - it was one of the old favorites, the one that Isabel loved.

UNIQUE

On the first day of school, it was evident to the teacher that Alfred Hazelwood was competitive and most eager to learn. Miss Sherwood was delighted. The boy, only eight years old, set an achievement standard for all the rest of the grammar school class, and Miss Sherwood was able to introduce more instruction than usual. Near the end of the school year, Miss Sherwood told Alfred what a wonderful student he had been. She was a little taken aback by the boy's answer.

"I want to be the best," he said. It was a terse and even harsh response. The little boy seemed too young for such determination. Miss Sherwood felt uneasy, and she bit her lip as she listened, and yet she complimented him on his attitude. She did it simply because teachers are trained to urge students on; they are under no circumstances expected to encourage students to take life more casually. Still, later that day, she was angry at herself.

In junior high school Alfred "joined up" for the baseball team, and he was placed in center field by Coach Jones. The coach was surprised when Alfred caught up with him on a stairway - and made an odd complaint:

"I'm not happy in center field."

"What's wrong with center field?" asked the coach.

"I want to pitch," was the simple answer from Alfred.

"Well," said Jones, "that's all right, but everybody can't be the pitcher."

"No," answered Alfred, "but I can be."

The coach was impressed with the boy's determination but he demurred.

"We went through tryouts and Williams was chosen, so that's how we're going to play it."

Alfred persisted: "If I work at it, would you give another tryout?"

"We always keep our options open," the coach said. "So if you can convince me that you're better than the other guy, I'm willing to reconsider." Coach Jones walked away. He felt that he had given this boy enough time.

But within six weeks Alfred was back asking for a new tryout. Jones went along because he had a hunch that the boy might help him get a winning team. Following the tryouts, Alfred was named as a substitute pitcher. Not long after that he pitched a no-hitter and soon became one of two permanent pitchers.

The coach met him by accident after school one day.

"Well, you got what you wanted," he said to Alfred. Of course the coach did not reveal that Alfred's rapid promotion was precipitated by an alumni reunion. There, the principal and the alumni had made it abundantly clear to Coach Jones that they wanted nothing but winning teams. They didn't say it directly to the coach, but everything they said to each other and everything they did screamed out the same message.

And now in casual conversation, the coach was justifying the reassignment on the basis of Alfred's demands, but he got the inevitable answer:

"I guess I did get a chance to pitch, but am I going to play most of the games, or is Williams going to do it?"

That question was irritating to the coach, so he answered obtusely:

"We'll play it by ear," he said tersely.

It didn't turn out that way exactly. Alfred Hazelwood's relentless pressure on Coach Jones payed off; he pitched more than three-fourths of the games.

The coach was in for another surprise. It came when he accidentally sat next to the principal during their lunch hour.

"You've got quite a boy on your baseball team!" the principal ventured. The coach knew whom he was referring to immediately.

"Yes, Alfred Hazelwood has become quite a pitcher," he rejoined.

"No, no, I don't mean his pitching," was the principal's unexpected response. "That Hazelwood boy has just been ranked second in the class in academic standing, yet he remains a participant in all kinds of extracurricular activities. He's very competitive, you know."

The chess club met one night a week in the lunch room. It was an entirely different world than that of the athletic teams. The room was filled with participants - all but one were boys. You could tell they were chess players at a glance. There was the type with oversized glasses, and others with old fashioned very small eyeglasses - no ordinary glasses. And then there were the small nervous types who couldn't sit still and bit their fingernails. But even more curious was another type, the kind who never looked directly into the faces of other people and always said slightly inappropriate things - but was very good at chess.

As Alfred Hazelwood walked into the chess club room looking tan and athletic, the members decided that he was not the chess type; they quickly discounted him as a real competitor. They were right, but only for the first six months. After that Alfred rose steadily in rank until he had become one of the top players. He had, as always, read books, asked experts for help, and played hour after hour. He was often seen all alone at a chess board trying out his strategies. No one snickered now as his large frame sauntered back and forth in the club room.

But even now, the complete dimensions of Alfred Hazelwood's ambition were not apparent. It was not until much later, following his graduation from college and after attending an investment training program, that the full scope of his determination became evident. As a young broker he savored early financial success and, with it, the power to manipulate money and people. His closest associate, Herbert Wilkins, talked with him about it after witnessing Alfred's meteoric rise:

"You've come a long way in a short time," he said.

"Yes I have," answered Alfred, "but I must not let up now."

"Aw, come on," interjected Herbert, "you can afford to ease up. Why can't you start enjoying life a little? And when are you going to get married?"

The rejoinder was simple and direct:

"I enjoy women, but it is not essential to me to have someone there all the time." But a few years later, as Alfred's income became enormous and his houses more imposing, the number of available women multiplied, and finally he did get married. He acquired a very attractive wife, Meredith, who managed the social events necessary to allow Alfred to increase the number of clients for his firm.

Meredith was a wan, beautiful, and keenly sensitive creature. She understood Alfred well. They seemed very happy and possessed everything that Alfred wanted, and more than Meredith needed.

One day Herbert Wilkins was visiting when Alfred was called away suddenly on urgent business. Before leaving he turned to Herbert:

"You don't need to leave. Stay and talk with Meredith."

Herbert stayed, and he and Meredith talked - and he stayed and stayed, and they talked and talked. They had never been alone before, and early on in the conversation they realized that they were embarking upon revealing much about their private lives. It was Herbert who made the first revelation: "I'm almost ashamed to admit it, but I live in complete admiration of your husband, Alfred." He thought Meredith would be delighted by the remark. Instead, she had a hesitant expression, and then she spoke:

"Things are not always as they seem."

That remark surprised Herbert and made him respond accordingly: "Whatever do you mean by that?"

Meredith was hesitant again, but she and Herbert

were now bound in one of those confidential moods in which people say more than they intend.

"There's another side to Alfred," she ventured. A moment of embarrassment followed. Herbert was not sure if he should enter into this surprising revelation, and Meredith wondered if she had been imprudent. But she had a repressed need to share the information and he remained curious. Meredith spoke again, this time with even more startling news:

"Alfred is a tortured man."

Herbert stood up abruptly, clearly reacting physically to news that shocked him; after all, this was the man he idealized. But after standing, he felt awkward since he was not leaving and had no reason for his new stance. And so he moved toward Meredith and sat down in a chair much closer to her, almost as a physical expression of their new relationship.

"I don't understand," he said perplexed. "Alfred has everything anyone could want. He is highly successful, he is admired by friends and respected by enemies, and he has wealth, status, and a wonderful family. What else could he want?"

Meredith looked pensive and resigned. She began slowly:

"Well, for one thing, he's never really had me." She paused, and then reconsidered what she had said and corrected the impression. "Not that I didn't give myself to him in every way. But, a man like Alfred doesn't know that joy must be shared. He thinks that joy is something that you get for yourself. Frequently, when he finally decides to talk to me, he says, 'this will only take a few minutes.' Often, it takes even less time than that. What I'm trying to say is that he never takes the time to really talk with me. He just talks at me. I think he could communicate with me very effectively, from his point of view, by just giving me messages in print."

Then she continued slowly: "Day after day, year after year, he struggles with a need to be the best at everything he undertakes. For that reason he's very good at many things, but there is always someone else who comes along and does just a bit better. Then too, he's always looking over his shoulder, wondering when that someone will overtake him. Alfred is like those people who are never satisfied with anything they can achieve easily. By his own definition of success, he is bound to battle constantly with a goal he can never completely attain. So there is no rest for him, and no rest for me."

Dumbfounded as he was, Herbert believed that he must ask the question:

"Haven't you pointed out to him that there is no need to be number one at everything?"

The answer was quick.

"Of course I have! And he knows it, and he often plans to reform, but from deep inside him the need wells up again. He also has another trait common to gifted individuals - an expectation that other people should peacefully give him all the time and energy that they possess."

Meredith was wound up now, so she couldn't stop talking:

"Alfred's greatest ability is that, whereas the rest of us see opportunities best after they've passed us, he sees them before they have arrived. But he sees so many of them, he can't rest. When success is too constant, it becomes a failure, you might say."

In the months that followed, Herbert tried to convince his friend Alfred that his obsession with success and superiority was foolish. But Herbert was not completely convinced of that himself, so he was not very effective. Alfred seemed to be thankful for the advice, but the restlessness of his drive would burst forth from some part of him that he could not resist - or even identify.

Herbert watched as his friend struggled in the midst of greater and greater successes. But since nothing satisfied him, Alfred used a common remedy that never works. He sought more and more power, and he grasped for more and more money; and with each success the demon within him was temporarily assuaged. But soon the craving returned, and then he would hunt again the elusive quarry.

If Herbert had been of a different turn of mind, he could have ignored his friend's situation; instead he became extremely preoccupied with it. He began to talk with his wife, Harriet, about it. She was a small attractive woman with dark eyes and high cheek bones. Sensitive and considerate, she was always willing to talk about Herbert's problems. At first it was just casual conversation. But soon they realized that their perceptions of Alfred were quite different, and their frequent disagreements were unsettling to Herbert. Harriet was quite cool about the whole thing because she saw Alfred as something quite outside herself. But soon she understood that Herbert was disturbed and much involved in the question of success. He wanted it as much as Alfred, but totally lacked the motivation and the energy. So he longed for something that he could not have. Eventually, Harriet understood that her husband was going through some kind of identity crisis about his own success, or the lack of it. Herbert was threatened. He wanted to be admired.

One day he expressed it frankly. He looked fixedly at his wife and blurted out a statement:

"Frankly, Harriet, I always had the impression that you secretly admire Alfred."

Herbert's lips were tight; he was a little afraid of the answer. But Harriet answered without hesitation:

"You don't understand,do you? Of course I admire Alfred. Everybody does. But I love you because of who you are, because you are unique."

"Me unique?" asked Herbert. "I'm the most ordinary guy in the world."

Harriet smiled wanly:

"You still don't understand. Alfred is the finished product of his school and his society. He learned to win at baseball, he was near the top in academic endeavors, and he pushed his way to the highest ranks of chess. But some years from now a psychiatrist may be telling him to be himself and take life more casually."

Harriet paused, but then she wanted to explain herself better, so she continued:

"I admire only some aspects of Alfred's character, and I wouldn't want to be married to him for anything in the world. Did you know that when Meredith was preparing to marry Alfred, she used to say that she would never want to forget any of the seemingly insignificant details about her marriage. Little did she know that she was one of them.

"And when I say that you are unique, I mean that every human being has something special and different about him or her - and that's what we should like ourselves for!" It was a strong statement, but her last sentence went right past Herbert. He wasn't ready for it, so he didn't really hear it. As the months went by the subject of Alfred came up often, but without any change in their positions. Harriet saw Alfred as a worldly success but a questionable personal success; Herbert remained in total admiration of Alfred. He wished he could be like him, but he could not. The possibility of being satisfied with himself for his unique qualities alone, and without the great approval of others, made little impression on him. And so it all continued that way. It would have stayed like that forever except for one thing - a new event broke into their lives.

It began one day as Herbert entered the brokerage firm where he and Alfred worked. He found all the staff quiet and huddled into little groups.

"What's going on?" he asked the first secretary he met.

"You haven't heard?" she answered.

Herbert made a guess: "The market has taken a fall."

"No,not that. Mr. Hazelwood has been locked up in his office and won't come out. They know he's in there because someone saw him go in, but he won't say anything and he won't unlock the door."

Everyone was now gathering around Herbert. They knew he was closer to Alfred than anyone else, so they expected him to do something. Herbert went to the door and called out to Alfred. No answer. He tried again. Still no answer. Finally he turned to the crowd:

"Call security and tell them to bring a pass key."

Soon a man came up with the key. Herbert told everyone to go away; he would go in alone.

Herbert turned the key in the lock. He opened the door slowly and took one step inside. The blinds were drawn and the room was dark. For a few minutes Herbert just stood there. He had a feeling that something was about to happen, but it didn't. A moment later Herbert took several steps forward, and then he noticed that at the far right of the enormous office there was a ray of light coming through a defect in the blinds. The sunlight made a single beam that reached the middle of the room. And then Herbert saw it!

It was an ominous black shape that broke the only ray of sunlight in the room. The large black shape reached from the ceiling toward the floor. At first it looked like a large black coat on a hanger. But then Herbert's eyes got used to the darkness, and he could really see it. It was the body of a man hanging from a beam in the ceiling. It was Alfred!

Herbert staggered from the room. The others went in. There were the usual exclamations and scattered ideas about what to do. As soon as the immediate decisions had been made, Herbert pulled away. He could not stand the office or the people. He excused himself from work and went home in a daze. His whole system was disturbed. He had to go home to Harriet.

She was busy installing curtains and surprised to see him. He collapsed in an easy chair; he didn't know how to tell Harriet the news. It was partly the shock of the whole thing, but it was also something else. After all, he had been completely wrong about Alfred. Harriet had obviously understood the human values involved better than he, and her theory about liking ourselves primarily because of our unique qualities suddenly took on more significance. Finally, he told Harriet about Alfred.

She stopped her work and came to his side. She said it was a terrible thing. She did not refer to their many discussions about Alfred, but she acted very much as if this was the expected outcome. Yet she said something different.

"I never expected a man like Alfred to kill himself by suicide. I thought he might eventually kill himself by overwork, but I didn't think he was self-destructive like that. He often attacked other people, and he worked too hard, but suicide is more like giving up." After saying that, she just sat calmly in a chair.

By afternoon Harriet was back at work installing curtains; from time to time she made soothing remarks to Herbert who sat once more in the same easy chair, unable to do much else.

Herbert looked at his wife more closely than he ever had, and he remembered their past conversations about Alfred. It had only been a matter of rhetoric at that time. But now the vision of his friend's body hanging from the ceiling made him really hear Harriet's words for the first time. She had tried to tell him that every human being should like himself for his unique qualities, not because he gained wealth or power. And at the time that she said it, Herbert had heard the words, but he had not fully grasped their significance. Nor had he accepted the idea and made it a part of his life. Now he was puzzled about how Harriet had come to understand this aspect of life so completely, so simply. Finally he asked her the question:

"When did you think this all through? I mean the realization that a person could actually die because of a failure to accept the idea that you must like yourself for your own unique qualities, not because of power or the approval of other people."

"I don't know", she said airily. "I always thought that."

Then, as if by an afterthought or a generous impulse, she added another thought: "I guess some of us are lucky. We come to that perception of life simply, as if it were the first attitude that we adopted. Other people just can't accept the idea. They have to experience a heart-rending shock before they really see it. But the answer is the same for all of us."

Herbert stood up quietly, calmer than he had been all day. He had never thought of himself as unique, and it felt good. He walked slowly over to his wife, and he kissed her on the forehead.

"You're unique too, do you know that?" he said.

MERETRICIOUS

The inn at the side of the ocean was Victorian; its elegance retained the grandeur that Americans associate with their distant past, although the personal heritage of most Americans is far more modest, and only an elite few really enjoyed the graciousness of those times.

John Van Heusen was born in the third generation of such gracious living, and although his own abilities were only modest, he retained the attitudes, and some of the capital, of the previous generations. He remembered the night he sat in the handsome lobby of the ocean-side inn, when the optometrist entered with his wife. One knew immediately that Mr. Travison must be one of those self-made men who could boast a great business success - and so he could. He owned several highly lucrative optometry shops, and the cash registers of these shops exerted an evident effect upon Mrs. Travison's couture. She was clearly the one to watch and was unremittingly successful in catching every eye.

But within John Van Heusen, the spectacle of this woman created a certain revulsion. Never in his experience had anyone so completely represented an entirely material sense of values. The gaudy and brilliantly colorful prints of those expensive dresses, the low-cut and provocative blouses, the enormous rings and pendulous silver ear rings, the bright green shoes, and the dyed silver-blond hair, all attested to a person without taste, or even a sense of propriety. The outrage it created within Van Heusen's youthful soul, however, was also due to the expression on the faces of the Travisons. Hers expressed a complete sense of assurance, a message that she represented complete social success in the very midst of a mediocre world. His was smugness and satiated satisfaction for having acquired wealth, and a wife whom he viewed as everyone's desire. Nothing would have pleased Van Heusen more than to have "topped" them in some way, or to have seen someone else who surpassed them at their own test of success.

John Van Heusen's youthful arrogance spared him the difficulty of any introspection. He did not need to wonder why the Travisons' self-satisfaction provoked such a violent reaction in himself. Nor was it necessary for him to realize how hard the man must have worked in order to achieve what he did. Mrs. Travison's own success, apparently passively attained, might well have been mixed with early deprivations and patient support of her man. But none of these questions interrupted Van Heusen's critical view or the adverse remarks that he shared with others. As the years went by, Van Heusen returned many summers to the shore-side inn and to its Victorian comforts. The clientele remained as constant as its high-backed wicker chairs and its glowing wooden panels. The expression of old wealth included nineteenth century values in people who still dressed for dinner. In its conservative aloofness this society remained apart from Mr. Travison and his wife, except to greet them politely without the warmth of human recognition. In short, this society treated them very much as Van Heusen did. It accepted them just enough to believe in its own tolerance, but never so much as to include them as part of itself.

It was most remarkable that as the years multiplied and Van Heusen's perspective grew, the possibility of compassion within himself, and certainly within the clientele of the old inn, did not grow at a pace which might compete with their rate of aging. So, years later, the annual visit of the Travisons was met with the same response as in the early years. The cool guarded hand-shakes were tendered properly and without hesitation. And the meaningful exchange of glances and more blunt remarks, just after the Travisons passed by, continued as an ancient ritual. Often John Van Heusen wondered why the Travisons persisted in coming. Were they totally oblivious of the evaluations so freely given, or was their greater wealth a shield that fully protected them? After all, they remained among the richest people there, and perhaps they saw the responses around them as signs of jealousy that reinforced their sense of success. And yet they must have known. Even if they did not hear the words, there was an aura surrounding their passage of which they must have been aware. It was summed up for Van Heusen one morning, when, after the Travisons walked through the lobby, he heard one of the newer guests asking an older client of the inn what she thought of the Travisons. The answer came in a single word. The elderly dowager looked serenely at her new friend and deliberately answered using a single word; the word was "meretricious". The regular clients of the old inn and Van Heusen had now known the Travisons for eleven years.

And after eleven years it was all so easily summarized, this total evaluation of the Travisons, into a single word.

At precisely three-thirty in the afternoon of Van Heusen's twelfth summer vacation in his familiar surroundings, he experienced a shock for which nothing could have prepared him. The vacation had begun much as always. The release from the busy winter season was ever the first pleasure. But recognition of the familiar and dignified surroundings was an equally rewarding experience. Ensconced in those deep comfortable chairs, Van Heusen gazed slowly about, steeped in the deep glow of woodwork reflecting light from hundreds of crystals hanging from the ancient chandeliers. The heavy draperies muffled the sounds, and only a rustling of gowns signalled the passage of familiar faces as the same old guests renewed acquaintances.

But this year a strange and shocking sight was to break upon Van Heusen's consciousness. It appeared at first casually, as a new pair of guests entered the opposite side of the elongated lobby. It was a woman sitting in a wheelchair pushed by a man with graying hair. As they came closer, Van Heusen could see that the woman must be the victim of Parkinson's disease. Her left leg and arm were partially immobilized by rigidity. There was a rhythmic tremor of the arm and hand. Her face was distorted, with flatness and loss of all spontaneous expression - as if a mask had been placed over that once beautiful face. Van Heusen stared dispassionately at the unfortunate woman, with the detachment that has come to us all from having witnessed many such distracting scenes in the course of life; and he accepted the attendant misery readily, as most people accept tragedy that affects many persons other than themselves.

But slowly, eerily, like some horrid nightmare, he began to recognize the face. As if hidden beneath a mask, the features emerged, as they etched upon Van Heusen's consciousness the awful truth. The face, the person, could be no other; it was Mrs. Travison. As the wheelchair approached, Van Heusen saw a greeting forming upon half her mouth, and beneath the mask-like face a vain, but gamely forced, smile. Her dress, as always, showed the expensive material, covered with the large colorful print of cheap design and very questionable taste. The man, slowly pushing the wheelchair was a rapidly-aged Mr. Travison. His expression, tired looking, remained none the less serene, and his every movement was directed to meeting her needs.

During the following week, Van Heusen observed, as unobtrusively as possible, the huddled pair passing by the halls and lobbies or sitting alone in the dining room. The pattern was consistent. Mr. Travison, remarkably dedicated, would patiently help to feed his wife, help her from the wheelchair to more comfortable seating, and read to her from magazines; indeed he responded quickly, but gently,to her every need. She, in turn, looked upon him adoringly and generated repeatedly the distorted smile which she directed mostly toward him - but also toward the guests in the old inn. Hour after hour one could see them sitting on the old veranda looking out at the pounding of the surf on the beach below.

The responses of the guests to this tragedy took many forms. Most of them displayed humane concern for people who had been so struck down by adversity. It could not, therefore, be said that the guests were calloused; far from it, most of them overtly extended themselves to express sympathy and concern. But nor could it be said that the wide divergence of social values between the Travisons and the well established clientele had suddenly melted in the light of human tragedy. The well established social positions protectively held, by all the guests and the Travisons alike, remained inviolate; indeed with fear and tragedy, the positions were held more and more desperately.

After that, as the days of summer came and went, Van Heusen would rest again and again in those deep and comfortable chairs, basking in the security of his established social class. He even slid his hand, from time to time, along the deeply varnished wood of banisters and center tables. The glow of the subdued lighting and the rich curtains and heavy carpets all attested to the values he shared so deeply with his old friends amongst the returning clientele.

But as the days went by, Van Heusen experienced an inner turmoil that he had never felt before. Incertitude turned to anxiousness, and anxiousness became restlessness as he surveyed his own life with its modest accomplishments. Tortured by self-doubts, he tested other clients of the old inn to see whether in view of the tragedy, they too, were racked by introspection. But they remained comfortably detached. And Van Heusen's uncertainty grew to agony. In the end he sat night after night in the lobby, deprived of his ancient comforts. The new questions kept pouring in upon him. Had his own life been worth as much as he originally believed? Had he achieved even as much as Mr. Travison? What were these ancient social standings that had so long protected him?

And so now when evening came, he would sit looking hopefully in the direction of the entrance to the lobby. There, an image of Mrs. Travison appeared, the way she was when she was young and full of life. He saw her there again, with that brightly flowered gown and the barely covered bosom, and that long flowing blond hair about her neck and shoulders. And yes, he even searched for the haughty air, the false sense of pride, and the confident smile. In one of those full length windows that faced upon the porch, he thought he could see her with her husband - gaudily beautiful as she was. But in the fading light, he imagined that the rich evening tones showed the Travisons and the old guests there together. And he thought he could see them reconciled, in such a way that their humanity overcame any difference in taste, or class. And this recapturing of a mythical past, a past that never was, spread over all to enlighten in that ancient Victorian window the darkness of its panes of glass.

INSPIRATION

Father Fenwick came to Saint Mary's Church when old Father O'Donnell retired. There were so many accolades for Father O'Donnell, the beloved priest, that many people believed he was irreplaceable. It was, therefore, a considerable surprise that within six months the young Father Fenwick was fully accepted. Soon, most of the talk about the old priest faded, and there were people who even said that Father Fenwick was the best priest they ever had, although no one said that in the presence of the senior parishioners.

What was the secret by which Father Fenwick achieved his extraordinary success? One could of course point to all the new activities and the stirring homilies. There were also new social hours, field trips, and stimulating Bible discussions with social implications. And Father Fenwick was in the forefront of many community affairs with extensive interdenominational discussion groups and interfaith programs. But none of these reasons really accounted for the very intense personal response that he evoked.

For over seven years, Father Fenwick felt entirely fulfilled in his priesthood. He could stand high at his pulpit, the very embodiment of goodness and success. During the delivery of the homilies, a packed church was hushed in admiration. On Sunday mornings, even before he uttered a word, Father Fenwick could rivet attention to his personal magnetism. Tall and straight he stood, with power to spare, which he seemed to transfer to his flock. Women thought he was extraordinarily good looking. With his high forehead, aquiline nose, and expressive mouth, there was a strong masculine quality about him which women admired and men identified with. Yes, he could pause deliberately for a long time before he uttered the first word of the homilies - and this delay would only increase the anticipation of his congregation. And then the sonorous sound of his voice would come ringing clearly in the rafters; or his voice was suddenly subdued in confidential sanctity. So, for seven years, the byword of this priesthood was success.

But then suddenly it happened! Not so that any of his parishioners would notice. It was all an internal and very strange event for Father Fenwick. His words were about the Virgin Mary, but his eyes were upon a young woman in the third pew. He had observed her before with respectful admiration. Now he experienced a powerful emotion, a feeling of love, or perhaps more accurately a sense of desire. At first it seemed like a passing thought, but to his dismay he soon realized that he could not put it out of his mind. Of course the emotion that Father Fenwick experienced had not developed in an instant; he had recognized a certain personal attraction for this woman since she began coming to the church six months before. But, it was at this moment that the depth and overwhelming nature of his emotion had suddenly reached his consciousness. In a few minutes he was able to reject the idea as unfit for a man of the cloth. But during the second paragraph of the next page of the homily, there was a recurrence of the preoccupation with a certain amount of imagery, now insistent like an illusion, or even a hallucination. No matter how hard he tried to blot it out, the unwanted image returned at irregular intervals.

When the service was over, Father Fenwick stood at the door shaking hands with his parishioners. A senior member of the church praised him for the homily:

"Very important message, Father, very important."

Father Fenwick felt vaguely insecure. He did not remember any part of his spoken words, even though he knew and recalled easily the details of his written homily. Reassurance came from the repeated compliments of the parishioners, but it remained shocking to Father Fenwick to know that he had been so distracted by an aberrant preoccupation. His discomfiture increased when he saw standing before him the comely young woman from the third pew. She grasped his hand and complimented him on the Sunday message.

"You deliver all homilies with so much feeling," she said. And then she added something even stronger:

"You're an inspiration to us all!"

Father Fenwick was relieved that he could look at her now without experiencing any untoward preoccupations. He was completely in control, and he made a few learned elaborations on the homily.

"A message is partly intellectual," he said, "and partly an expression of how deeply we believe."

As he finished his sentence she seemed to glide away from him as other people came forward to greet him.

But the memory of the experience would not pass away so easily during the rest of the day. He was particularly disturbed by the stark contrast between her perception of him as an inspiration and his vision of her as an object of desire. Father Fenwick reassured himself with the thought that lust, after all, is a natural human trait, and that everyone has passing ideas which one cannot be held accountable for. But never before in his life had he felt anything with such intensity or persistence. Nor had a thought recurred so uncontrollably.

Father Fenwick's experience was disturbing to him precisely because he was a good man and an honest man. He began to wonder whether it was appropriate and proper for him to remain a priest, while experiencing such a preoccupation about a trusting parishioner.

On four subsequent Sundays the congregation included that young woman, always in the third pew, and Father Fenwick was much relieved that there were no untoward thoughts. Indeed, he began to wonder if he had made much too much of the whole thing. The memory did not quite fade, but now it lacked the vivid quality that had so alarmed him.

However, a month later, just as his homily became more animated, Father Fenwick gazed at the third pew and, to his utter consternation, the preoccupation returned. And when he tried to dismiss it, he could not. He was imprisoned in his own thoughts. And Father Fenwick's consternation was made much greater because this time the fixation was translated into an odd breakdown of his performance. He was making a reference to "the Father and the Son and the Holy Ghost," but he almost replaced the last few words with a new phrase inappropriate to his main theme; he almost said "the Holy Virgin." Fortunately it didn't quite take place; he said " the Holy Vir.." and then corrected himself to " Vir---Ghost."

People realized that Father Fenwick had made a slip of the tongue, but the intended, or unintended meaning, and certainly the association, escaped them entirely. So, at first, he thought it turned out all right. But was it really all right? For Father Fenwick it was not. For him the obsession, which he now viewed as an ailment, had returned. It hovered over him like an ancient specter, or more like a young sorceress. He considered the latter seriously. If it could all be viewed as an evil outside himself, he would be much relieved. But Father Fenwick was an enlightened man who did not entertain belief in literal interpretations of the devil, so it was impossible for him to convert the event into an inquisitorial investigation of someone else's sin, as others had done successfully a few centuries before.

Father Fenwick was now very frightened because, for the first time, he realized that the illusion could force him into an error in speech. Indeed it had already done so. What if something worse were to take place? What if he said some terrible thing in public?

As he stood in the church hall following the service, he saw the young woman across the room. She wore a velvet skirt and a white blouse slightly open at the neck; he realized what an attractive woman she really was. Slowly, irregularly stopping to talk with other people, she was making her way across the room toward him. Whether willfully, or by chance, she came closer and closer until her body touched his arm. And then she turned, seemingly surprised at the accidental contact, and she grasped the hand of the priest.

"I want to thank you, as always, for your message today." She continued softly without hesitation or restraint: "You may have noticed that I always sit in the third row."

Well yes, indeed, one would have to say that he had noticed. But he answered obtusely:

"No, I hadn't really taken note."

Then the prevarication disturbed him, and he immediately corrected: "Oh yes, now that I think of it, I did notice you there."

Her soft voice continued:

"I sit there because I can hear you more clearly, and more important than that, I get a stronger transmission of the intensity of your message." Father Fenwick felt rescued by an immediate response that came to his mind:

"I can understand that; the acoustics in the back of this church are not everything that one would hope for."

Father Fenwick felt concerned about what the conversation might lead to next, but other people fortunately interrupted, and she moved toward another group of people with her usual grace.

It was not until Father Fenwick returned to his apartment that the impact of the latest events were pressed upon him. His ethics, his very life, and certainly his religious calling were directly threatened - at least he believed that. He repeatedly reminded himself that the same kind of obsession in a layperson would carry little significance; but for him, it seemed like an expression of hypocrisy. He could find fewer and fewer themes for his homilies that did not, in some way, reflect upon what he viewed as a loss of righteousness. Finally, in desperation, he concluded that he must seek help. But, could he trust any person with his secret? He considered normal channels; he could talk with his bishop. But he did not feel secure about the long term effects upon his standing in the Church. Of course the bishop would accept it in confidence, but would he ever regard him in the same way again? Then too, Father Fenwick knew everything the bishop would say to him. He would begin by saying that we are all human beings, that it is natural for us to have certain desires. After that, he would elaborate upon the special calling of a priest, and how his marriage to the church and his acceptance of God replaced the earthly desires. Indeed it was part of the beauty of his calling that denial should be a part of it. And the whole discourse from the bishop would be presented in an honest, but in the case of this particular bishop, slightly sanctimonious way, which would make Father Fenwick uncomfortable. Besides, he had already said all these things to himself, and it gave him no relief. As for seeing anyone else, a professional person, it would rob Father Fenwick of his self-image as the one who is the confessor and advisor. Then too, it would take only a word to spread rumors in his flock and change, or even destroy, his very special relationship with them. But finally the pressures were too strong upon Father Fenwick, and he decided that he must seek help. So he turned toward a man whom he instinctively trusted; he settled upon his family physician, old Doctor Meade.

"Good to see you," was Doctor Meade's jovial

greeting, "but I never expected to see you here in the office. Hope you're not sick."

"No, I'm not sick, but I do have something to discuss with you."

"Ah yes, well, I have been slow in making my contribution to the church, but it is my full intention to do it."

"That's not it at all," Father Fenwick fumbled on, "I need to discuss a personal matter."

But Father Fenwick could not go further. When he looked at the distinguished old doctor, and reminded himself that the doctor was still one of his parishioners, he could not bring himself to disclose the emotion that plagued him. Instead, he told Dr. Meade that there was another man in the parish who had a psychological problem; this allowed Father Fenwick to describe a modified version of his own difficulty.

Old Doc Meade laughed. "Why I get things like that all the time," he said, "and I just enjoy them." But then Doc Meade became serious:

"You know, I believe that having temporary infatuations, or even imagery about an object of desire, is normal. And these feelings and thoughts are abnormal only if they seriously disturb the person having them. So I would tell your parishioner to relax and put it out of his mind. If you think he needs help, I'll give you the name of an excellent psychologist, a Doctor Blaine."

The conversation with Dr. Meade had, from the outset, been quite soothing to Father Fenwick. After all, Dr. Meade had expressed how normal it was to have such thoughts. But slowly, and then day after day, Father

Fenwick's obsession returned.   He remembered that Dr.
Meade had said that it was not normal when a preoccupation or an illusion was emotionally disturbing to the
subject, and disturbed he certainly was.   Furthermore,
Father Fenwick understood that Dr. Meade did not really
understand his problem.   As much as Father Fenwick
respected Dr. Meade, he knew that the doctor had none of
the religious compunctions that a priest lived by.   The
doctor was motivated to remain faithful to his own wife
because he felt a happy and satisfied commitment to her. It
was not because of any religious, or even ethical,
constraints. So Father Fenwick perceived correctly that
Doc Meade could not be of any real help to him.   As for
the possibility of seeking out the psychologist, it was not
exactly the proper channel for him to follow.   But, finally
he concluded that he must seek out the psychologist and
request his total confidence.   He would go see Doctor
Blaine. Surely a trained psychologist in a nearby town
could be relied upon to be strictly discrete.

As the priest approached Doctor Blaine's office, he
felt an element of nervousness, but he remained determined
to seek help.   As he walked toward the office, he decided
upon his approach to the interview. He would lay out the
facts in a forthright manner, man to man.

At Dr. Blaine's office, the receptionist led Father
Fenwick into the office to meet the psychologist. In every
consideration of the outcome of an interview with a
psychologist, it had never crossed Father Fenwick's mind
that he might come face to face with what he beheld as he
stepped into the office! He literally stopped and, standing
there foolishly, made an effort to formulate some sort of

greeting. Father Fenwick's total embarrassment had come about because Dr. Blaine was a woman, a very attractive woman at that. It was not so much that Father Fenwick was prejudiced about women professionals, as it was that he had carefully prepared himself mentally for a conversation with a man. So now the preparation was of absolutely no use. In a man to man alk, he had imagined that the doctor might well have ; dmitted to a similar experience. But a woman was another matter. The approach would have to be entirely different. Father Fenwick even considered avoiding the issue. He began by describing himself as having certain uneasy feelings, a mild nervous state, during the presentation of homilies. Doctor Blaine stated that this was quite normal and even believed that a little tension was beneficial to public speaking.

"I completely agree with you," Father Fenwick responded. He knew this interview was entirely nonproductive so far. But the good Father could not depart from the office without dealing with the principal issue. The anxiety created by his obsession was greater than any social or personal inhibition. So, finally, he presented the real problem. Dr. Blaine gave no evidence of surprise or shock, which was a great relief to Father Fenwick. She was really a very engaging person and spoke freely about her professional experience with other problems of this kind. For about one hour they exchanged ideas and feelings regarding such preoccupations. Father Fenwick had become quite relaxed, and he felt a profound relief that he had not experienced for many months. With more tranquility, Father Fenwick was able to contemplate Dr. Blaine more objectively. She was unquestionably a very attractive woman. Her hair was long, jet black, and only slightly wavy. It was clearly the product of hours of grooming. The shape of her eyes was extended slightly laterally by eye shadow which shaded the eyelids - then continued in a thin line into the creases at the sides of her eyes. She had an inconspicuous nose, but she had very full and sensuous lips.

At this moment, Father Fenwick believed it had been good fortune that brought him to a woman psychologist. He believed, for the first time, that his private obsession had been shared with a woman. And that in itself should furnish some relief.

But suddenly, there was complete consternation! As Father Fenwick's eyes perused the doctor's classically beautiful face and shapely body, he began to realize that it was possible, just possible, that he could develop an attraction for this woman as well, very much as he had for the woman in the third pew. He could not prevent himself from forming certain highly personal images of her. And the preocupation was extreme in the vivid illusions that it created. And now Father Fenwick knew that his obsession had reappeared. Far from relieving his obsession, Doctor Blaine had become the object of it. She still spoke to him about his problem, but nothing that she said had any meaning now. Poor Father Fenwick discontinued the interview; he said he might come again, but he knew that it was a useless exercise.

Back in his living quarters Father Fenwick became more and more desperate. Running away seemed like the only outlet for him now. But where would he run? And what would he do? It was old Doc Meade who, accidently, and without any perception or insight into the problem, furnished a temporizing answer. Father Fenwick had run into him on the street. Doctor Meade's usual direct and laconic style led the conversation:

"You're not looking well, Father; why don't you make some change in your way of life?"

That was it! Father Fenwick grasped at the escape. He would carry the suggestion a step further - and try to be reassigned to a new parish. Much to his surprise, a mere hint to his superior led to an appointment to a new church. But it was not exactly what he had in mind. The church was located in a very wealthy area with many actors and actresses in the parish. There were also many wealthy corporation executives, and even prominent politicians. Father Fenwick had grown up in a protected but poorer environment. And, at this moment in his life, he had visualized and hoped for simpler surroundings.

What happened during the next few years and in the time that followed, became, many years later, engulfed in Father Fenwick's mind amidst those large chains of memories that later summarize a whole lifetime of experience.

It was only now, in old age, that Father Fenwick, sitting before his fireplace at night, was able to talk about his ordeal - with an old friend. The fear of being exposed was now gone since he was retired from his church. David, a former scientist, sat quietly in the firelight.

It was Father Fenwick who raised the issue:

"David, have I ever told you about my obsession?"

"Never knew you had one."

"Well, I did," said Father Fenwick, and he proceeded to tell his story, so well hidden, for so many years. David was too old to be shocked, but he was curious.

"So tell me, what did happen after that? I mean in the new parish and after that."

"Well, it all seems very short and simple now," said Father Fenwick. "The new parish was really located amidst the 'jet set'. I was surrounded by extremes of wealth and behavior. I witnessed for the first time what licentious living can be. My confessional was a shocking revelation, and finally I even had indirect offers of more intimate relations with women. I think some of these women derived their pleasure from such proposals to a priest - as if they wanted to pluck something sacred and make it their own.

"In time, I learned some important things about my own character. And although I must admit that I was often haunted by my emotions, I never yielded to my desires."

At this moment there was a pause in Father Fenwick's story, as if he realized that this interpretation was too simple. Then he continued slowly:

"I think that the new parish gave me a new point of reference about what evil really is. I began to realize the rigidity of my upbringing and my code of ethics. I could see more clearly the differences between normal desires and the choices we make as a result of them. And I understood that I was imperfect, but not truly evil or guilty.

"Would you believe where I got my greatest lesson? It was when an old alcoholic wandered into the church and told me all his troubles and degradations. He was so open about it that I innocently spoke about myself. I even told him about my own ailments and my guilt. At first he was surprised, but then he said something that stuck with me ever since. He said 'I think if I were you, I would be a little kinder to myself.'"

David was still curious.

"But what about the preoccupations and the illusions ? Did they go away just like that?"

Father Fenwick was slow and thoughtful now.

"No, they never really left me. I would go to church, and sometimes I would develop again a powerful feeling toward one of my parishioners and even experience some of the vivid images that were so uncontrollable. But one thing was different now. I saw myself in the context of all human behavior. I was neither superior nor totally righteous, but nor was I evil, and within my new self I was more fully a part of my community."

"I agree with the assessment that you adopted late in life," David said. Then he continued:

"Since I'm not very religious, I hesitate to quote to you from your own Book. But as I read it, even without any religious conviction, the difference between good and evil was defined in the Garden of Eden. And the problem with Eve was not that she had been placed there, or that she was tempted by the apple. The problem with Eve, was that she took it."

TEMPTATION AND SANCTITY

James Fosdick attended the school of architecture, and he lived in a room near the school. With very little money for rent, he had located a room in a converted apartment. There were seven other rooms, each rented by different occupants. His location was between two rooms rented by women, one young and the other one old.

The young woman was the first to come by to greet him. A slightly full-bodied person, with a plain face but inviting eyes, she stood in the doorway of his room and chatted. She peppered him with questions about himself; he felt he was being evaluated. In the following weeks she came by periodically to visit, or she would ask him to drop by her room, presumably to talk. Sometimes when he went to visit her, he noticed a pipe and tobacco on one of the tables.

The old woman, who rented the room on the other side, was a furtive person. For the first six weeks, he never saw her; none the less he was aware of her because frequently he would hear her door open and later close - and then there was a shuffling of feet in the hall. Whenever he opened his door she was gone, but soon after he closed it the shuffling would return. There was a slight sense of mystery in all this coming and going, without any personal appearance on her part.

One night, he caught a short look at her as she headed for the staircase. It was merely a glance, and the image he retained was not so much of a woman as of a pile of clothes. She was covered by a purple velvet gown, and bird feathers curved over her head from a velvet hat. He was certain that it was she, as he heard the now familiar shuffling gait.

He began to think more about his situation - about being ensconced in a room between two women. He had a casual acquaintance with the young one and no knowledge of the other one. But in time he got to know her as well - not by meeting her, or talking to her, but merely by the pattern of her coming and going. Evidently she had no job, for she was in at all hours of the day. No friends or relatives came to see her; no mail was in her box. There was not even a newspaper delivery. At night he could see a little light under her door. Occasionally the sound of an old record player was just audible, and popular romantic music of the early nineteen hundreds brought images of old movies to mind. The rest of the time was total silence, except for the shuffle of her feet - and at times a rustle of clothes or papers.

Late one night as he sat reading a book, he heard the familiar shuffle, but this time it came closer and finally stopped in front of his door. He waited, listening. She shuffled away again, and he heard her door close. About ten minutes later he heard her door open again, and the footsteps moved toward his door and stopped once more. Soon she left.

The next morning as he opened his door, he was surprised to find a small package lying on the floor. He picked it up thinking it might be for someone else, but then he saw his full name written on the package. The wrapping paper had an elaborate blue floral design, and as he began to open it, a strong odor of lilac filled the air. Inside the wrapping he found a small black book; it was a Bible.

Perhaps he should go thank her, he thought to himself. But his instincts warned him that this might be unwise. She was, after all, a very odd person. And even if she were innocuous, was not the relationship best left as it was ? If this was an imaginary service she was rendering, and if she did it without identifying herself, was it not her wish to keep a distant relationship?

A few weeks later at nearly one o'clock in the morning, there was a knock at his door. He had a premonition - that it would be the old lady. He opened the door, but standing there was the young woman from the other side. She was, very obviously, dressed only in a night gown and slippers.

"Can I come in?" she asked, as she walked casually past him into his room. She explained that she was unable to sleep and needed someone to talk to. He was ready for sleep, but decided to make use of the time by having an evening snack. He began peeling an apple.

"Would you like one of these?" he asked her.

"No thanks, I'll watch you" she answered. "I really like the deliberate way in which you peel that apple and the way you eat," she continued.

"I wasn't aware that I did it in any particular way," he responded, in an offhand manner.

"But you do," she insisted, "and I love the way you enjoy every bit of the taste of it."

The conversation continued in this rather strange and aimless way, and soon it occurred to him that he had a busy day coming up. He must bring this one to an end. And he thought this could be easily brought about by a simple remark:

"I'm afraid I will have to get to bed now, because I have to be in school by seven."

It seemed like an effective, though slightly direct way, of ending the visit; he was not prepared for her reponse.

"Can I stay?" she said, with a dreamy look in her eyes.

He understood her meaning, and he realized that this was a question that most men under most circumstances would most like to hear. For some reason it affected him negatively. Somehow she was less attractive as a result of that overt impulse bluntly directed toward a relative stranger.

"Well, I'll tell you," he blurted out, "I've had a very long day and another long one almost ready to start, and I've got to call it quits."

"But I don't want to go," she persisted, "and I didn't say you couldn't go to bed."

Now he was even more determined that she must leave. They exchanged several more remarks, and finally she left with a wan but unsatisfied expression on her face.

After she left, he went to bed wondering if he was very virtuous or very foolish. And for James Fosdick the question was more than rhetorical. He had grown up with very religious evangelical parents and a strict code of behavior. But at this time in his life, he was struggling with his own desires, and these were frequently in conflict with the strict Biblical teachings and injunctions of his parents. So this woman's overt offering of her body, with its appeal to desire and guilt, was not something that he put easily out of his mind. In the darkness he imagined what it would have been like to take this woman and make her his own.

As he lay there trying to get to sleep, he heard the old woman's familiar shuffle, but this time it definitely stopped at his door. A small piece of paper was pushed under the door, and the footsteps could be heard again, leaving. Turning on the light once more, he recovered the small piece of paper; it had a single sentence on it, "Jesus saves, sin no more."

Had he sinned? He had actually done nothing. But, his evangelical past reached out for him with accusations of sin as it pertained to his mind and his intentions, as it related to venial sin. During the next few weeks, the shuffling at his door came every night, and each time a small slip of paper was placed under the door. Most had a verse from the Bible. Many spoke of sin. He felt as if he had been placed in a modern Garden of Eden - temptation on the left and sanctity of some sort on the right. From his distant Sunday School past, two verses from Genesis kept coming to his mind:

"And the Lord God said, Behold, the man is become as one of us, to know good and evil: and now lest he put forth his hand, and take also of the tree of life, and eat, and live for ever:

"Therefore the Lord God sent him forth from the garden of Eden, to till the ground from whence he was taken."

For many days James Fosdick felt as if his past and his precepts were grasping for him again, as if his recent experiences obliged him to be preoccupied with the forces of good and evil. But gradually the Biblical verses became more distant; he began to confront his ethics according to his own standards and not those of his parents, and his definitions of good and evil became softer. And when the time came for action, for a decision regarding his relationship with these two women, he made a simple choice. He moved to another room, in a different building far away.

THE ALABASTER MAID

The physician saw her first in a clinic - one of those well-meant places where people are forced to wait for hours on end. She looked very much like a doll, a beautiful six year old girl. Her mother recounted the medical history. The child had many ailments in her short life, and the mother was concerned that she did not act like other children.

"She doesn't warm up to people, Doctor."

As the mother spoke, Dr. Eaton looked at the fine features of the delicate child. She smiled a little at him, and her pretty sparkling eyes were fixed on him. After this clinic visit the physician did not see her for many years. But he remembered often the wan smile and the beautiful face, but most of all he remembered the pallor of her delicate skin.

Eight years later, the girl was brought to Doctor Eaton again. She was now fourteen years old. The mother sat in the chair next to the small office table, and the physician faced her. Dr. Eaton was aware, even then, of a strange quality in the third being in the room. It was the child who sat respectfully in a corner at the periphery of his vision. Appropriately, as the mother spoke, he would look at the patient from time to time. It was the common patronizing fashion in which he scrutinized his patients as the medical history unfolded. This was not entirely a casual habit, but rather one which facilitated a personal evaluation as he observed their general appearance, posture, movements, and changing expression.

"She has never been like other children," the mother recalled. "When she was a baby, she was perfect, and we were very happy with her."

The mother had apparently forgotten those many ailments she had recounted during the initial visit to Dr. Eaton, but he had recorded them carefully on the chart that now lay before him on the desk. The mother continued:

"She was a good baby, too. She was quiet, and ate and slept good. But when she became older, she always complained of funny feelings in her body. Once, she said there were like-snakes crawling around in her stomach. She's different from other kids in other ways, too, but I don't know what it is. We're hoping you can tell us what it is."

Doctor Eaton barely listened to the mother's words as all his senses became engrossed in the scrutiny of his patient. The child sat seemingly attentive, yet looking straight ahead with a fixed posture of the head and neck. For her age, she appeared to be unresponsive to the situation of being in a doctor's office. Never a word was volunteered. In this immobile and passive state, communication between the mother and the physician alone prevailed. And yet when he looked at the girl she seemed to stare directly back into his eyes or, as he later recalled, beyond or through him.

He asked, then, to have her undress, so that he might examine her. A brief color came to her cheeks. It was gone so fast that, if he had not been looking directly at her, he might not have noticed. Throughout the examination she sat with strange composure. Dr. Eaton began to question her: "Do those funny feelings throughout your body bother you very much?"

"Why yes they do, at times."

"But is it bad enough that you would want something done about it, like an operation for instance?" He was trying to test the severity of the symptoms.

"I wouldn't want anyone operating on me; to tell you the truth, I don't even like anyone to touch me."

Later, Dr. Eaton explained to the mother that he found no physical ailment. But in an effort to make the interview more casual - and also because of an impulse - he added a remark:

"You know, she's the prettiest girl we've had here in a long time."

The mother responded with a smile, but the girl looked as if nothing personal had been said.

When she left, Dr. Eaton remembered her for a long time. It was more his custom to put patients out of his mind as they stepped from the office, and to remember them again only when the chart was re-presented to him on a subsequent visit. But this girl was different. It was perhaps her fair complexion or her extremely fine features. And then there was that rare beauty. Perhaps it was even more that remarkable face. It underwent subtle modifications without visible changes in expression - it had a mystical quality. At times, from her eyes, he thought he saw friendly recognition, and he tried to smile at her. But then, that mask-like expression appeared to form over her face, and she was again a doll - pale, quiet, beautiful.

Three years later, another call to Doctor Eaton's office was from a mother.

"Can I bring my daughter to you for private consultation? You've seen her before in the clinic."

It was she again, and seventeen. Her beauty was now breathtaking. The pallor of her skin was as before, but the lips were painted red, and the eyebrows were dark and long, contrasting sharply with the transparent look of her eyes. Her body was perfectly proportioned. Doctor Eaton felt a strange and unfamiliar emotion. Had he ever seen such a beautiful woman before? She's so exquisite, he thought. His slight loss of composure made him uncomfortable.

Repeating all the medical history with long digressions, and many personal additions, the mother spoke of her daughter's behavior.

"She stays out too late. It's not good for a young girl to stay out so long - a mother worries. Could I speak to you alone, Doctor?"

She described her daughter's relationships to boys:

"Sometimes she seems too interested in them, and other times she acts cold to them. She was even seeing a married man for a while. But no matter how many boys or girls she knows, she never has anyone she treats like a real friend. I can't even communicate with her. I wish you'd talk to her yourself, Doctor. Perhaps you can talk some sense into her."

He was soon alone with the young woman. He spoke of her health and the results of her examination. Doctor Eaton's forehead was cool and slightly moist. She was still and perfectly composed, even detached. At times her eyes focused directly upon his. Was there cruelty there? In other moments, he felt that personal warmth was reflected in her brief smile, but the expression and the eye contact faded as fast as they came.

Dr. Eaton was usually direct with his patients; he brought himself to it slowly this time.

"Do you have a special boy friend?" He spoke jovially.

"Not a special one," she responded laconically.

He persisted: "But maybe you've had some that were a little special."

"I dunno, they're O.K.."

"Well, perhaps you have some good friends among the girls in your class?"

"I know a lot of girls."

No matter what Dr. Eaton tried, he could not make any real personal contact. She revealed no inner feelings. But was she hiding them, or were they just not there? He felt like shaking her to evoke a genuine response, but he knew only too well that it wouldn't work.

The office visit ended with plans for early follow-up visits and psychiatric care. But as on previous occasions, the patient and her mother never came for the follow-up visits, and again he did not see her for some years. From time to time he remembered her. Even at home as he sat before the fireplace, he would put his book down, and then he would see her pale face and skin, the long black eyelashes, and the red lips. A mystical sensation came to him, and then a brief sense of shame. He recognized that the face and body were like those he had often seen in daydreams. It was his idealized sense of beauty. Where was she now, and what had become of her?

Two years later, a call to his office was from a young woman. It was she. About to be married, she wanted her fiance to know about her condition, about what she now called her illness and the strange feelings in her body. She wanted Dr. Eaton to explain it to him.

"He has to understand me - and it's hard for me to tell him in words. Would you explain to him?"

Doctor Eaton wasn't sure he understood her problem himself. But after agreeing with her request, he turned to face her. She was now a fully mature woman, and he spoke more freely with her than before. He felt sure that in this new relationship he would understand her better. Now she would no longer be an image, a doll, but would become fully alive and be like other young women about to be married. At first, he felt relieved as he spoke to her. But near the end of the office visit, when he finally turned eagerly for some responsiveness on her part, he saw the pale statuesque beauty, the full red lips, and the clarity of her bright eyes; but she seemed again to fix her eyes on a distant site, looking more past him than at him, and he knew once more that she would not be fully with him.

After this visit, she never returned to his office, and her mother never called. The physician assumed that she was, at least for the moment, better. Occasionally, he would remember the strange quality of her face - that haunting expression.

But Dr. Eaton had a busy practice, and, in time, he was able to almost put her out of his mind. Among the other patients that he saw were the many mentally ill people at the local psychiatric hospital. Dr. Eaton had no psychiatric training, but he attended that hospital to serve as a consultant in internal medicine.

It was during one of Dr. Eaton's consulting days that he was met by the hospital director, who ushered him into his private office because he wanted to review a case with him.

"It's a very sad case, Dr. Eaton," the director began. This young woman is schizophrenic. She made a sudden attempt to kill her mother, her husband, and her child. They all seem to be all right, although her child does have a very marked pallor. I want you to see the patient because, aside from her mental problems, she has complained about many intestinal symptoms. We did all kinds of X-rays as well as other studies."

Dr. Eaton reviewed all the studies, but he could find no evidence of organic disease. An orderly was called who ushered Dr. Eaton to the floor for psychotic patients.

The key to the room was turned; the physician entered with his customary assertive manner. The lighting was poor. He sat down near the small bed, reached for the patient, and turned her gently toward him.

Suddenly, Dr. Eaton's calm professional air was lost. He looked with dismay at the unreponsive human form. As the orderly turned a bright light upon the patient's face, Dr. Eaton's breathing became hesitant and a great sadness overwhelmed him as he sat immobile.

He recognized the marble white skin of the patient and the beautiful face. Her head and neck were motionless. He looked at the perfect features, the full lips, the pointed nose, and those long thin eyebrows, extending over slanted haunting eyes. Both eyes were fixed directly upon him. Now he felt a ghastly certainty; it was she. And after all those years in which he had repeatedly tried to use his medical skills to help this human being, was this all that was left?

A desperate need to save her caused Dr. Eaton to reach forward and lift her toward him, as if to bring her back. He looked at her eyes and saw a faint expression of recognition, deep in the moist eyes. He was sure that if anyone could reach her now, it was he, he who had known her since childhood. But then her face changed again; she seemed to look through him, or past him. It was like the face of some mystical icon from a forgotten past - and the skin was alabaster white.

The physician laid her back slowly, and he watched the gentle movement of her breathing.

"She's gone," he said, "she's gone."

The attendant leaned forward, holding her wrist.

"No, Doctor, her pulse and breathing are fine."

"Yes," said the doctor, "I know, I know."

WANTING MORE

"I suppose the trouble was that John Whitcomb
wanted more." It was Reverend Bigelow speaking to the
moderator of his church, Estelle Brown. But Reverend
Bigelow was in a contemplative mood, and he was speaking
as much to himself as he was to Estelle. They were sitting
in the church office having a cup of coffee after reviewing
the church budget. They often sat like that and enjoyed it.
Today they were reminiscing about previous church
problems, and that led them to John and Dorothy
Whitcomb's divorce. Estelle had not had access to John
Whitcomb's private life, so she was curious:

"Was John happy with his wife?" she asked, trying
to look casual.

"Oh sure," was the response. "John Whitcomb was
always happy with Dorothy. He had two lovely children, a
mansion, and a top level position as vice-president of an
important financial firm. His wife, Dorothy, was not
beautiful, and she was certainly a little stout, but I think
you would agree that she was comely, with a lovely smile.
Also she was hard-working, considerate, loving and smart."

"So why in the world would a sane man do anything
to lose such an ideal existence?" Estelle sounded angry as
she continued: "Honestly, sometimes I think men seem to
have no judgment whatsoever when it comes to things like

this!"

The Reverend Bigelow was less agitated and more thoughtful.

"I don't see it like that, although I spent dozens of hours trying to talk him out of it."

"Well!" exclaimed Estelle, "I wish you would explain it to me. How did it all get started?"

"I suppose it would be all right for me to talk about it now," the minister continued pensively. "You see, John Whitcomb woke up one morning and looked out his window. There, on the sidewalk across the street, was what he described to me as 'the most beautiful woman in the world'. Of course she wasn't just standing there alone. There was a moving van there, and men unloading her furniture. She was moving into the house directly across the street.

"John had known that the house had been sold. And he was not particularly interested in knowing what kind of family would buy it, because John was all wrapped up in himself and his career. But as it turned out, there was no family moving in, just one woman alone. And what a woman!"

Estelle was annoyed by the Reverend's exclamation. "Don't tell me she had you enthralled too, like all the other men."

"No, I would not say that. But you must admit that Sherry Conover was a strikingly beautiful person, and that she had a charming personality. Besides that, John Whitcomb had never before really known one of this new breed of women executives. He thought they were all business, like the ones he had met at work. He was overwhelmed when he discovered that a woman as successful as this one could also be warm, flexible, charming, and even seductive.

"So I think when he first looked out his window at her, he was taken with her beauty. But later, when he met her, he was overcome by her other qualities. And he proceeded to compare her with his wife. And as he started watching Sherry regularly from his window, I think he began wanting more."

The explanation did not placate Estelle: "I'll never understand this thing that suddenly overtakes an otherwise perfectly sensible man!"

Reverend Bigelow avoided looking at Estelle directly but he countered gently:

"I've seen it in women too. It's true that it appears to be less frequent in them, but a few years ago one of our parishioners with a husband and three children suddenly had a visit from an old boyfriend. He was now a doctor. Would you believe that she was so stimulated by the visit that she came for counseling? She was precipitously certain that she had made a terrible mistake in not accepting him twenty-two years previously when he had proposed to her."

Now Estelle was on a new trail. She wanted to know who the woman was, who was so tempted. But Reverend Bigelow would not yield on this one because the woman was still a member of the church. So Estelle returned to the first topic:

"I never knew the Whitcombs very well. They left soon after I came to the church. Whatever happened to them?"

"It's actually a fascinating story," Reverend Bigelow declared. "No matter how hard I tried to dissuade him from it, John Whitcomb pursued his exploration of Sherry Conover. He kept going over to help her with the house and the lawn, and soon they were jogging together. One thing led to another, and eventually he announced that he wanted a divorce. At first Dorothy couldn't believe it! She was so good, so innocent, that she was sure it was all a mistake, something unreal that happened to other people. But finally she became resigned. The divorce was completed and John Whitcomb married 'more', that is, he married Sherry."

"Did you ever see him and Sherry again after they moved away?" Estelle's curiosity was rising again.

After a pause, Reverend Bigelow responded: "For a long time I heard nothing. Then one day about five years later, I was invited as guest minister in another town. During my sermon I was casually looking at the people sitting in the pews, and there he was in the congregation!

"He was sitting next to a rather homely woman. I assumed she was not actually with him, and I wondered where Sherry was. But after the service, when I was not so preoccupied with my sermon, I saw them again. And much to my consternation, I realized that this homely woman was Sherry. She was completely transformed. I can only describe her as lumpy - lumpy all over. She had fat cheeks, wide hips, and a protruding abdomen. She had completely let herself go. Apparently she had stopped exercising and ate too much."

Estelle had difficulty concealing an element of satisfaction. Finally she said it:

" Serves him right."

" That's not very Christian," the Reverend chided, in a friendly manner. Then he continued: "You haven't heard the most amazing part of this story. Of course Dorothy had moved away too. I suppose she wanted to get away from everybody and try to start a new life somewhere else. I was genuinely concerned about her and I liked her very much personally, so I made it my duty to write to her frequently. Gradually her letters became more cheerful, and one letter suddenly announced that she was married again. She continued to write and invited me to visit if I were ever in her new town. One day I went to a religious retreat near her, so I called her. That's when I was shocked to discover what an amazing story this was!"

"Good grief," said Estelle, "What are you going to tell me now? I'm afraid to ask."

The Reverend Bigelow had a whimsical expression on his face. He seemed to delay the next part of the story, as if he savored the experience. Then he told her what he saw:

"When I rang the bell at Dorothy's house, it was she who answered the door. My surprise must have shown, because Dorothy said airily 'Yes, it's really me.' What I saw was a Dorothy who was also drastically changed! She was no longer stout, but slim and svelte. Her personality reflected her satisfaction with herself, and she explained the diet and the exercise program that were responsible for the transformation. When we reached the living room, she introduced me to her new husband who was good looking and apparently very much in love with her."

Now The Reverend Bigelow stopped, and he

watched Estelle. She was quite definite:

"All I can say is - it serves John Whitcomb right. I'd go a step further. I think it was divine providence."

He answered her very deliberately, almost in a didactic manner:

"I don't see it so simply. Life and people are more complicated than that. John Whitcomb was not an evil man, nor did he ever want to be cruel to Dorothy. It was more as if something was just happening to him - as if he had not willed it so, but had come to a point in life when he thought that life had passed him by in one respect. He believed there must be some great experience out there that he would never have, and that Sherry alone could furnish it. I've racked my brain for a solution to these problems, but I still don't know how to handle them. There is one thing, though, that I'm pretty sure of."

"What is that, Reverend?" Estelle asked. He countered with a question of his own.

"Do you remember that when you were a school girl and you became infatuated with someone, the feeling usually faded after a while?"

"Sure," said Estelle more brightly. "I saw one of those boys a couple of years later and I wondered what I had ever seen in him."

"That's just it," said Reverend Bigelow. "In my experience, unrequited infatuation does not last."

"Yes, but what could they do different?" asked Estelle.

"They could wait. Do nothing, fight nothing, but just wait. Mature love grows against all odds, but infatuation grows only when it is constantly fed, when it is impulsively gratified. If only people would wait a year or two to make decisions, they wouldn't make such foolish choices."

They sat after that without talking for a long time. They seemed lost in private thoughts. There were reasons in both their lives for the interim.

Estelle was one of those attractive women who never got married. No one, including herself, could understand why. Underlying her pleasure in the presence of Reverend Bigelow was the way his character nearly met her requirements. Of course, he was married, so a personal relationship was out of the question. But time together was possible.

Reverend Jonathan Bigelow was very good looking. He was powerful in the sense of a great inner force. He dominated the church by virtue of his wisdom and quiet strength, by an attitude that brooked little opposition, but never seemed to invite open clashes with other people. So Estelle, without ever admitting that she was attracted to him personally, was well aware how close he came to the ideal that she had never found.

Reverend Jonathan Bigelow, on the other hand, was happily married to one of those ideal minister's wives - the kind who meets the needs of a pastor and never competes with other women in the church.

Now The Reverend Bigelow and Estelle sat quietly, wrapped in thought about the personal implications of what they had been discussing in John Whitcomb's life. Suddenly they realized that it was an awkward pause in their conversation. Estelle blushed, and Jonathan tried to explain it.

"I suppose that 'wanting more' is common to all of us."

But then they sat quietly again. She searched more frankly into his handsome face. He looked a little bit away from her. Then they continued their discussion about John Whitcomb; it was the easiest thing to do. Estelle began again with a question:

"So what do you think John Whitcomb should have done?"

Jonathan looked a little more directly at her, almost tenderly:

"I guess he should have waited longer."

She searched his face again, but also answered simply:

"I guess that is the only thing to do."

THE BEAUTY TRAP

"Explain it to me," Al said. "I just don't understand it at all, and I've agonized over it night after night. Our daughter, Judith, is extremely pretty and a wonderful girl, but her beauty has failed her. I don't mean that she has lost any of her beauty, but it hasn't done anything for her life."

Al's wife, Ellen, didn't really know what to say. Finally she gave a weak answer: "We've been through it before, and there is no answer."

"I just don't buy that, Ellen. There has to be a reason, and it's our duty as parents to help her with it."

Al and Ellen Harper were once again trying to understand why their daughter had reached the age of thirty-eight and still was not married. It all came up again because Al had been sitting in his office when he overheard a conversation of two young men in an adjoining room; they were discussing Judith. What struck hard at Al was that one of the young men said categorically to the other: " That daughter of Al's, the one called Judith, is without question the most beautiful woman I have ever seen." And then the other young man agreed. Al had always believed that his daughter was beautiful, but this was the first time he had overheard such an extreme adulation from two young men, and since they were not aware of him, the reality of it was stark and convincing. So her extreme beauty was true, not just a parental prejudice, and it made the paradox of her lonely existence even harder to bear. And worse than that, Al knew that Judith was finding it harder and harder to bear.

Al Harper often sat at night in his easy chair unable to think of anything, other than his daughter Judith. He and Ellen had three daughters and one son. One of their daughters was a rather plain-faced girl who got married easily right after college graduation. She had not had many options, but her life was relatively uncomplicated, and her aspirations were realistic. She wanted and got a man who was reasonably good looking, considerate, and fairly successful in a small business. So he met her requirements, and they got married soon after they met. It was as simple as that. Al's second daughter was somewhat more attractive, had always had a boyfriend or two, and found herself a dentist, who could hardly be described as a scintillating personality; but he was safe, made a lot of money, and became a faithful husband.

But Judith was something else. Even in junior high school the boys could see that she was different. And from the start they were always around her. At first it was mostly to tease her, but soon they wanted to take her on dates. At that time Al and Ellen had worried about her, because they feared an escapade of some kind.

Once Judith was in college, the rumors filtered home to the parents that she was surrounded by young men. Of course they had expected that. But once again they worried that something would happen. Throughout all this time the Harpers never even considered the possibility that Judith would not find a man to marry. Their only concern was that she would find one too soon, that she would get pregnant, or that she might elope or make a bad choice.

Judith herself was quite satisfied in college. An intelligent girl, she had an interest in English and composition. She thought she would like a career as an English teacher, perhaps in a college; and beyond that she dreamed of becoming a writer. As for the young men who surrounded her, well, she took them for granted - the way she always had. They were always there, and by now she had understood that almost all of them wanted her. So she knew that if she was ever inclined to marry, all she had to do was say, "yes".

It was fun for Judith to go to the college library, find one of the great works of literature and sit at one of those solid oak tables and read. Her genuine interest in literature was thus satisfied, and without any effort on her part she could simultaneously participate in an occasional flirtation. Judith would sit there in her prim way, her classical profile causing all male students to look, or even pause, as they passed. Since Judith was bright and truly interested in English literature, she would become lost in her reading for a time, and then she would become aware of some young man who deliberately selected to sit at the same table. She would enjoy that too, and even give him inviting glances, but then she would turn her attention back to her work. What fun! It was a repetitive cycle, a sliding in and out of the world of books and the excitement of flirtation. When she lapsed into one of her being-admired phases, she could practice those wiles that come so easily to good-looking women.   Sometimes she would pause and apply a little lipstick, or pass her comb through her lovely blond hair, or readjust her clothing. And when she wanted to tease a particular boy, she would pull her skirt up a little, as if to sit more comfortably.

Of course the evenings were either spent at parties or in occasional study interrupted by phone calls from suitors. Week-ends were largely fun, but Judith was a student, and she made it a point to reserve parts of Saturday and Sunday for her studies.   This in no way interfered with Saturday night occasions, and even with social life on Sundays. So there was no question about it, college life was a complete success for Judith. She had the best of both worlds - a promise of a successful career and an active social life in which she was constantly at the center of all important occasions. After graduation Judith did well too. She was taken under the wing of one of the professors, who helped her obtain an instructor's position in the college. And the young faculty members, the men, behaved toward her just as the students had.   Even the Dean noticed her at one of the faculty receptions, and he stopped to talk and then introduce her to others as one of the school's recent recruitment successes.

So life was beautiful, and life was success, and life abounded with the pleasures of being admired and wanted. Al Harper and his wife knew all this, and they watched with pride and anticipation, this, their most outstanding daughter. It did not seem possible that anything could go wrong with this successful offspring. In fact one could easily have said that nothing did go wrong.   At least nothing happened suddenly.   But as time went by the

Harpers became gradually aware that nothing was changing. Judith continued in the same vein year after year. Once in a while Ellen Harper would question Judith by gentle hints regarding a possible more serious relationship with one of her many suitors. And Judith would pass it off lightly with a breezy comment:

"I don't need anything more, Mom. I'm happy the way it is. I've got everything I want." Well, of course she was right, although she was not taking into account the effects of aging. How could she? She did not know that aging begins the moment you are born; but it is only recognized later. There had been no interruption of Judith's happy state after she finished school because it was still due to a college mentality, persisting as it often does after graduation. And it would continue for a time. Failure to establish a mature relationship with someone could be defended on another basis. After all, she was now a young career woman, and everyone knows that it is not necessary for them to consider marriage. What's wrong with living alone? The attraction that Judith had for men naturally led to a few more intimate relationships. And the first man she accepted could only be described as a young Adonis. And the second one was much the same - tall, handsome, suave, bright, and ambitious. As a result she was the envy of many less perfect women who would have given much to attract either of these men. The affairs were, however, less than satisfactory. And Judith was too much of a person not to realize that there must be a possibility of achieving something more permanent, or at least nobler, than these quickly formed and easily dissolved relationships.

So for the first time Judith was not as certain of her total satisfaction with life. She realized that living alone was all right only to the moment when you begin to think about it very much. When she was a young girl living out a career alone she was happy, but lately it was more the appearance of happiness. And when her mother hinted again that it was getting late in life, Judith did not answer as glibly as before:

"I'm bearing that in mind, Mom," she responded.

Indeed there was a creeping sense of incertitude, an uncomfortable feeling that her world was no longer perfect, even though she still had everything she had always had. What was different was her perception of life and that wanton rider who travels along our side even before we know him, that unwelcome guest, that harbinger of age.

Progressively, without the loss of any of her beauty or ability, or her popularity, Judith now knew that the world was more complicated than she had realized. She groped for an answer but could not find it. She still had men of every kind at her beck and call, but none of them satisfied her expectations.

One day Judith came closer to understanding herself, although as it turned out, it was not close enough. It came about because she began observing women her age who were not married either. In many of them the reasons for their remaining single were obvious. They were too tall, or too fat, or they were ugly or disagreeable in character. But some were none of these, and they interested Judith the most. They were the ones most like her, the beautiful ones who were also smart and successful. They were the ones in which beauty appeared to fail. What were their reasons? Judith decided to ask some of them directly.

But this search led Judith nowhere. The results were exemplified by Alice Worthington. Wealthy, gorgeous, pleasant, and successful, she was much like Judith. She too was unmarried and not happy about it. Their conversation started well enough:

"Alice, I'm curious. Why have you stayed single?"

Alice began with the defensive routine, explaining that her career took all her time, that with her many interests and activities she didn't really need a man. Then she said that all men seemed to lack the character traits that she wanted. But after a while she too wanted to seek an answer from Judith. So the pretenses were dropped and Alice made the first admission:

"Of course, although a modern woman can live alone, I have begun to realize that five to ten years from now the apartment could seem very empty."

On that they both agreed. They were also thinking of something else, but they didn't say it. They were beginning to recognize that the unspoken miseries of daily living, the uncertainties and the fears, would be easier to bear if one had a good partner at one's side. But, to avoid that admission openly, Judith and Alice agreed that one could always talk to another woman. By the end of their conversation, however, they knew that neither of them understood what was wrong with their situation. So how could they be of help to each other? And when they parted, that lonely feeling was back. So another woman was not a solution. And after trying several other beautiful women of the same kind, Judith realized that they all knew that something was wrong, but none of them could quite put a finger on it. Once again Judith was left frustrated.

Bewildered, she turned to her father. He began happily because he thought Judith was "coming around". He told her exactly how to solve her problem.

"You've got to get around. You need to find the right man, that's all."

"But Dad, you usually complain that I get around too much, that I see too many men."

That made Al a little less sure of himself, so he responded with impatience.

"Well, I mean that you must not have been going out with the right ones."

Judith knew very quickly that her father didn't have any answers. He neither understood her problem, nor did he have any helpful suggestions. And he closed their father-daughter talk with an optimistic remark:

"I'm sure that now that we've had this little talk, you're well on your way to resolving your problem. A pretty girl like you shouldn't have any trouble."

Then he hugged her and rushed off to work. Judith was depressed. She was so depressed that, for the first time, she resolved to seek help, to see a psychiatrist. Through a friend's recommendation she found a Dr. Spinel.

Dr. Spinel was a quiet, analytical, slow-talking person, so Judith soon took over the conversation. That was the way Dr. Spinel wanted it, but it would have been that way anyhow because she was more outgoing than he. For six months she saw him once a week, and the interviews went well from her point of view since she did all the talking. And Dr. Spinel was pleased too, since he was getting well paid, and the patient seemed satisfied. At the end of six months, however, it dawned upon Judith that Dr. Spinel had not done or said much of anything. This realization and the cost of the visits finally prompted Judith to ask for his input.

"You've pretty well heard my life story, Dr. Spinel. Can you tell me what my problem is?"

Now he was forced to participate. He gave a short, well-rehearsed speech, presented in his careful analytical style:

"Let me give you the benefit of my experience with unmarried women. First let me say that there is nothing wrong with remaining unmarried if the person is happy about it. But you are clearly troubled by it, so it should be viewed as a problem. There are three factors that I believe can produce your situation. I will tell you what they are, and you must figure out which one applies to you.

"The first factor is the situation that exists in people who are incapable of loving anyone other than themselves. Think about the meaning of that carefully. There are many people who are attracted to others and think they are in love. But they think of other people as acquisitions. They care about people only in the sense of what others can do for them.

"The second factor is the fear of prolonged closeness. People who have this fear make many short relationships, but they are afraid of a commitment to a single person that they must see day in and day out.

"The third factor is observed in people who never understand that, in order to get along well with another human being, one must be prepared to give in a little more than fifty percent of the time. There are many people who are ready to meet a spouse half way on every problem, but it remains difficult to identify the halfway point. So, when they insist on a strict fifty-fifty relationship, they are always fighting over who needs to give in more. The answer, of course, is for both of them to be willing to give in a little more than half the time."

Dr. Spinel stopped talking and just sat quietly to see or hear her reaction. He was quite satisfied with his learned observations, even though they were not really original. But Judith didn't know that, so she was quite impressed:

"I've never thought about it exactly in those terms, and I think that will be very helpful for me." Then she breezed on in her voluble style, giving him multiple examples of what he had just said, as if he needed to have his statements illustrated to him.

During the next three weeks Judith tested the application of what she had learned against some of the men she was seeing. Slowly and depressingly, her perceptive mind began to understand that although there was some truth in what Dr. Spinel had told her, it did not apply to her. Not one of the three reasons given was really the problem that she faced. She just knew it. And finally, exasperated, she decided to turn to someone else. It was an old high school friend, a man who had quietly admired her, who had always been there when she needed him, but who never appealed to her as someone to love, as someone to be excited about. He was, however, faithful, considerate, thoughtful, and always concerned about her welfare. He was Robert Farmer. Judith asked him frankly if he was willing to give her several evenings to talk over a problem of hers. Of course he was pleased to do it, and they met in her apartment. Judith, who knew that Robert had always admired her, found it easy from this superior position to tell him about her concerns. She wanted to get his opinion, but she never dreamed that he would simply give her the answer. He said it very simply:

"I call it the beauty trap. It is what happens when beauty fails, not when it wanes, but when it fails to bring you any lasting relationship with a man. Surely you must know that you are a very beautiful woman - extraordinarily beautiful."

She answered frankly, not modestly:

"I know that men have always been attracted to me. But it has not brought me happiness, just entanglements. And that's the problem - no one seems to know why."

Robert looked at her longingly and seriously:

"Don't you have any idea?"

"No I don't, and the professionals, like the psychiatrist I went to see, don't know either. I don't think anyone knows."

Robert sat quietly but intently and then said:

"I think I know."

He said it so quietly that she almost went right on talking. But he had also said it with great self-assurance, so a few sentences later she stopped in the middle of a sentence and asked:

"Do you really think you understand it?"

"Well I'm no psychiatrist, but it all seems fairly evident from my point of view. I call it the beauty trap." He was repeating himself, because she had not seemed to pay enough attention the first time. Then he continued:

"I've noticed something about very beautiful women who never find the right man. They have such a wide choice of suitors all their lives that they naturally come to believe that they should select the very best man around. Not just a good man, but one who appears to be better than all the rest. They are trapped by their own beauty. Since everyone is at their feet, these women cannot settle for any ordinary man. Repeatedly, they look for the most handsome, the tallest, the brightest, and the richest man around; unfortunately they often also select the most dominant and aggressive man. So repeatedly they try to establish meaningful relationships with these dominant, aggressive males. And each time, they find out that after the initial excitement is over, these dominant men continue to dominate. And any woman who values her self-esteem does not want that permanently. So it develops into an impasse every time." He stopped talking and just sat.

Judith, for the first time in her life, did not take over the conversation again. She too just sat. The words had sunk in. Robert had said something that shook her to the very core. He had said something that from her very foundations she recognized as something real, not a series of theories like those of the psychiatrist. She felt uncomfortable, but she tried to parry:

"But all beautiful women don't have this problem. Many seem to fall in love and marry a man they are happy with."

Robert was ready for that too:

"All beautiful women don't have the same fatal attraction for very dominant agressive men, but it is a trap that they fall into more frequently than less attractive women. I think that people like you live with an illusion, the belief that beautiful people must be beautiful inside, and therefore desirable. But it's worse than that; you search out men who attract you because they dominate. And yet, of course, you don't want to be dominated for any length of time." She knew that Robert's theory was true and that it applied to her. She was still puzzled that this old timid friend should have come to it so easily.

"How in the world did you ever think of this so clearly? The psychiatrists don't seem to understand it, after years of study." He looked searchingly into her face, no longer wanting to hide his feelings from her. He spoke slowly: "I think I understood it because of you, and because of me, because I was always at one side of these events."

"How is that Robert?"

He responded with a question of his own:

"Have you ever thought of marrying someone like me?"

She knew, without his ever speaking of it, that Robert had always had a secret admiration for her. She took it for granted. Now that he asked, however indirectly, she had to make a response for the first time.

"I've always respected you, Bob. I just don't think you're quite my type when it comes to marriage. But I know you're better than I am in many ways."

He wanted to say more about himself, but he knew deep down that it would not lead to anything more, so he kept it general:

"Well, you see, you've just said it yourself. A

person like me makes a good friend for you, but I'm not the handsome, dashing, dominant man that excites you. When you go out to dinner with me, it's really the meal you enjoy most."

She tried to repair it: "I think you're a very nice looking person, Bob; I think we just don't quite match."

He wanted to say something like: "Don't you see that the reason I don't match is the very reason you have trouble finding a man you can live with? Your expectations exclude quiet, considerate, non-aggressive men." He wanted to say that, but he wasn't going to tell her again. So, eventually they parted quietly.

He walked slowly toward his apartment, in that resigned way he had. And Judith? Well, Judith was shaken to her very soul, for this was the first time that the truth had been said. She now understood the problem better than she ever had, and each time she went out with one of those attractive men, she could see more clearly the truth that Robert had spoken. So she had finally come to an answer, and at first it made her optimistic. She was on the right track. But the trouble with Judith was not gone. Weeks went by, and then months. And she tried to date men of a different type. And her father and mother kept introducing her to new men, men who had all the attributes that they admired, men whom they knew would be attractive to Judith. Of course they were successful and dominant.

Judith tried and tried, just as all the other Judiths in the world. She had a few exciting affairs with the men she admired, but she knew she would never want to be in their control every day. As for other types of men, she kept trying them too. But they bored her and she could not really love them.

And ever since, Judith has continued in her "beauty trap". In her most desperate moments, in her anguish, when she knows full well whom she really should marry, she tries again to make herself love one of those kind and considerate men - but then she is forced to say it to herself again:

"I simply cannot make myself love Robert, or any of the other Roberts in the world."

So Judith continues living inside that wonderful exterior, that beautiful face and body, that wondrous shell, that terrible trap.

THE FALSE MISS SWEENEY

He was thirty-seven and unmarried, and he was a poet who had achieved a moderate success in the publication of his work. Benjamin McGlathery accepted his mediocre success philosophically. He had convinced himself that the limitations of his popularity were the outgrowth of truth to himself and disregard for commercialism. But the results of his meager success in literature, whether due to truth in his work or inadequacy, made it necessary for him to hold a job as a salesperson in order to survive.

There were only a few hours each night when Benjamin McGlathery felt fulfilled in his mission in life - it was when he sat in his study, pen in hand, writing those verses which distinguished him from the other salesmen. There, in the solitude of his small room, he could imagine himself creating verses that would eventually bring him his rightful place in the world of literature. As he worked casually and comfortably, he would periodically put down his pen in order to pick up a book that held the ancient treasures of other writers. Instructive and entertaining, these creations often led to wide swings in. the emotions and moods of Benjamin McGlathery. He was a sensitive creature.

In the solitude of his own room, with an imagination larger than the room, Benjamin would enjoy a few special hours each day when there were no limitations upon his self concept. Separated from the menial tasks of the day and from the commands of his superiors, he would, for a few evening hours, reside in his own world of eloquent words and beautiful phrases - a world in which he alone was the judge of his own success and talents.

Benjamin's world had two compartments. One was the practical world in which he was a salesman, forced into physical contact with other people. He accepted them only as a necessary counterpart of existence, but never as members of his private world. The second compartment was at home in his study, where he controlled a world of imagination and poetry. Neither compartment truly allowed other human beings to break into his privacy. It had been like that for thirty-seven years, and would have remained that way, except for the arrival of the book.

It was a small black book that was sent to him as a trial offer by a publishing house. The book cover had a simple title embossed in gold letters. The title was "Poems from my Room", and the author's name was Elizabeth Sweeney.

Benjamin McGlathery was immediately attracted to the title which seemed like a description of his own life - and when he read the first poem, he was fascinated. The words flowed with gentle ease, and the sentiment was strong with penetrating insights. Benjamin was sitting in an upholstered chair with light streaming in from a window. As light began to fade, he turned on a floor lamp and continued to read. He could not set the book down. The lines seemed to speak to him, and of him, and about all the things that he cared about. He continued to read through the dinner hour. Completely immersed in the world of Elizabeth Sweeney, he knew that it was his world as well.

For the first time in Benjamin McGlathery's life he allowed someone else to enter into his secret world. And she entered through the words that she had put to paper, without even meeting him. During the next few months Benjamin read all the poetry by his new-found author. At first he borrowed the books from the library, but soon he purchased all the copies he could get, and after he read each one, he placed it carefully with the others in a row on a bookshelf he preserved for Elizabeth Sweeney's work. At times he walked past this bookshelf and slid his hand along the spines of these beloved books.

Gradually, something more meaningful began to happen. Benjamin believed that he had fallen in love with Elizabeth Sweeney herself. Of course that seemed to be ridiculous - to fall in love with a woman he had never met. Yet, he knew that this was precisely what had happened to Robert and Elizabeth Barrett Browning. And there was a special reason that made it more likely in McGlathery's case. A man like Benjamin, who had never loved a wo-man, but carried on a rich imaginary existence with literature, was particularly susceptible when suddenly his defenses were penetrated by a kindred soul.

Benjamin wrote a letter to Elizabeth Sweeney but never mailed it - he just filed it in his desk drawer. A week later he wrote to her again, and once more he filed it away. In this way he was communicating with his new love but maintaining his seclusion.

But one day, after re-reading one of her poems, Benjamin was suddenly moved by an uncharacteristic impulse. He stood up, walked over to his desk, pulled out his last letter to Elizabeth Sweeney, placed it in an envelope, addressed it and mailed it. He did it all without any expectation of a response. And sure enough, there was none. He wrote again, but still no answer.

In December, Benjamin was invited to a party. Although he usually refused invitations, he accepted this one because it was near the Christmas holidays, and many writers and editors were due to attend. It was the social group he admired most.

The party had the usual combination of drinking, noise, and pointless conversation. As Benjamin was introduced by the hostess, he hardly listened to the names she proffered, but suddenly he heard the name Elizabeth Sweeney. The woman the hostess pointed to was blond, attractive, and looking at him intently. So this was Elizabeth Sweeney!

Within a few minutes they were engaged in conversation. She was charmingly unassuming and immediately took a lively interest in his poetry. Benjamin expected her to say something about his letters, but she gave no signs of recognition. He assumed that she had forgotten, or that she had paid no attention to his letters. Perhaps she did remember but did not want to embarass him. They both acted as if this were their first contact.

In the weeks that followed, a lively friendship developed between them. Their relationship grew because she was outgoing and friendly, and because she penetrated his reclusive tendencies, drawing him skillfully into the outside world. And then, of course, she was so interested in his poetry.

Benjamin was puzzled, however, by her reluctance to discuss her own poetry. But he admired this trait because he identified with it; she obviously considered her poetry a very private thing, as did he.

Once, when they were eating in a restaurant, Benjamin decided to make an indirect reference to her work.

"You don't talk much about your poetry," he said.

She looked at him with a puzzled expression and countered with a question:

"Why should I?"

Benjamin was pleased by her apparent modesty, so he responded with admiration:

"I believe that you have written some wonderful things," he said.

She looked a little embarrassed but responded in her easy way:

"Well, apparently you know about my efforts at poetry, but I never considered them wonderful."

Benjamin was now overwhelmed by the combination of her talent and humility. She had no need for recognition; she was obviously selfless and, like him, produced her work privately and for its own sake. Benjamin imagined her as another Emily Dickinson, quietly rolling up her poems with a ribbon and filing them away in a drawer. Perhaps like Emily Dickinson she needed someone else to draw forth her talent and expose it to the world. But Benjamin determined that he would never challenge her privacy again. All his pent-up desires were released by his admiration and late-found love.

Within a few weeks Benjamin was catapulted into considerations of marriage. And, like other people long separated from social contacts, he became suddenly impulsive. He proposed marriage to Elizabeth and, much to his surprise, she readily accepted. They were married in a private ceremony, and he arranged to have someone read her poetry in addition to the traditional music and ceremony. Again Elizabeth amazed him. She said nothing to him directly about it, but she did express appreciation for all the additions he had introduced.

The first few months of their wedded life were full of happiness, as they always are, and she provided him all the human needs so long repressed by his previously desolate existence.

But there was one thing wrong. In the intimacy of marriage, he was sure that she would soon share her poetic inspirations, but she did not. After all, his love was initially based solely upon his empathy for her poetry and its emotional expressions. He began to feel excluded by her extreme reticence. And he was concerned about her sacrificing all her time to him, since she did not set aside any time to continue her writing. So, more and more he relinquished his vows not to intrude upon her personal endeavors, her creative spirit.

Finally, he decided that he must confront her. But how could he do it in a casual, non-threatening way. He decided to accomplish his aim by a gift. He took the best collection of her work, had it rebound at considerable expense in a handsome leather cover, and presented it to her.

She looked at the cover, felt it with her hands and

said:

"This is the most beautiful book I've ever owned." With that, she sat down, opened the leather cover, and looked at the front page:

"Oh my goodness!" she exclaimed. "I see why you bought this for me. The author is a woman whose name is identical to my maiden name."

Benjamin wondered what strange expression of modesty his recently acquired wife was now verbalizing. Was there no limit to her self-effacement. He made a few humorous responses to her strange remark, but she remained quite serious.

Gradually the smile on Benjamin's face began to fade. Slowly, incomprehensibly, fearfully, he began to understand the truth, the remarkable coincidence. But he remained incredulous. So, he asked her frankly to show him some of her poetry.

"Oh, you don't want to see that," she answered modestly. He insisted. She went to her room and brought back a little brown notebook. He opened it nervously. What he read made him feel a penetrating sense of emptiness, as if a major part of his life had just been taken from him. He looked at the pages of her notebook with disbelief. It was all a school-girl's sentimental prattle.

There was no way he could avoid it any longer. There had been two Miss Elizabeth Sweeneys, and one was now Mrs. McGlathery. He had married the false Miss Sweeney!

Benjamin was now overcome by a sense of unreality. How could such a thing have happened? But, of course, retrospectively, it was all quite obvious. Only the coincidence of identical names was unusual; her immediate interest in him and his poetry when they first met was only the expression of an admiring reader.

Benjamin McGlathery hid the awful truth from his wife. But he could not hide it from himself. Day in, day out, he suffered from his secret. And gradually it began to erode their relationship. Benjamin could not prevent himself from thinking that somewhere, out there, was the real Elizabeth Sweeney, the soul that he craved for.

As each day passed, Benjamin became more irritable. He even harbored certain feelings of contempt for his new wife, not because of what she was, but because of what she was not. And eventually, the inevitable took place. Benjamin began to drink too much for the first time, and he began to see other women. Poor Elizabeth understood that something was terribly wrong, but there was no way she could understand the reason. So, she concluded that it was her fault, that she had disappointed him. At night, when she was alone, she cried, but in his presence she always smiled and answered his impatience with love.

Their marriage became a very precarious union, and Benjamin spent more and more time with other women. But this activity, in itself, was quite remarkable for him, since before his marriage he had lived without any socializing with women. He was changed and more outgoing because of what his new wife had taught him. None the less he was frightfully unhappy.

The marriage continued, but it was moving rapidly toward disunion. Benjamin realized that divorce was inevitable. He became quite resigned to it, but did not quite take the necessary action.

A few months later an extraordinary event took place. Benjamin, without his wife, went to a gathering of writers and publishers. There, one of the editors of a magazine looked directly at Benjamin and asked bluntly:

"Mr. McGlathery, are you familiar with the work of Elizabeth Sweeney?"

Hesitant, Benjamin answered as nonchalantly as he could:

"I am familiar with her work, indeed I am."

The editor reacted enthusiastically:

"Well then, you simply must meet her. She's here."

Benjamin could hardly answer. He just stood. The editor was quick to continue:

"Come along, we'll find her." And he grasped Benjamin's arm, dragging him across the large room.

There, on the other side, Benjamin could see a woman; he knew immediately that it must be Elizabeth Sweeney, the real Elizabeth Sweeney. Sure enough, the editor was leading him directly toward her. Everything was happening very fast, and the editor introduced them:

"Elizabeth," he began, "I want you to meet one of your admirers." She liked to meet people who admired her, so she immediately launched into active conversation. She was beautiful, vivacious, witty, and obviously very bright. Benjamin was enthralled. This was the real Elizabeth Sweeney.

But the more Benjamin looked, the more he heard the eloquent English gushing from her lips, the more he became unhappy. After a while he began to drink.

Elizabeth Sweeney stayed next to Benjamin for a long time because she interpreted his silence purely as admiration. And, basking in this extreme adulation, she manifested more and more clearly her true character. Gradually, even in his slightly inebriated state, Benjamin began to see that she was egotistical, self-centered, opinionated beyond reason, and totally uncaring of anything that related to others. However, she repeatedly said that she remembered Benjamin's name from somewhere. Suddenly, she remembered that it was from the letters he had sent her. But far from expressing an apology for not answering, or a sense of gratefulness for his interest, she hinted broadly that she did not approve of his having written without first being introduced. After that, she talked about herself a while longer, and then she turned to someone else and was gone.

Benjamin made his way home, where he could hardly bring himself to a civil greeting to his wife. As early as posssible, he excused himself and went to bed. He lay there, eyes wide open, for a long time. But gradually he allowed the remaining alcohol in his blood to carry him off to sleep.

The next day he began to think again about the enormity of the events that had befallen him. The real Elizabeth Sweeney was certainly nothing like her poems, and this caused Benjamin new grief as he realized that his imaginary lover had never existed at all - yet she had inveigled him into marriage to someone else. This created a special irony in Benjamin's life.

Benjamin also believed that he must face the inevitable divorce from what had clearly become "the false

Mrs. Elizabeth Sweeney McGlathery". It was an uncomfortable existence. And throughout his tribulations, his little wife remained patient and supportive. She wondered always in what way she had failed. But she never blamed her husband, since she believed that it was a deficiency in herself.

The marriage continued in this way for month after month. Unhappy as Benjamin was, he still did not quite take the necessary steps toward separation. And, throughout his misery, Elizabeth was always there, loving and tending to his needs.

Then something happened! It was not anything that could be viewed as an event, but it was a very significant moment.

It happened one Sunday morning. Benjamin was sitting in the kitchen eating the breakfast of pancakes that Elizabeth had prepared.

Elizabeth, after setting up his breakfast, had gone upstairs to wash her hair. Now she had returned to the sunroom where she sat quietly brushing her golden hair in the sunlight. Benjamin could see her through the kitchen door, but she was unaware of it. This situation resulted in his calm and deliberate observation of his wife. Slowly, he sipped his coffee and watched her every move. For the first time, he was looking at Elizabeth - really looking at her. Her lovely long hair was streaming down over her shoulders, and the rays of the sun seemed to envelop her as if forming an elegant painting. But the real beauty that he saw was not due to her external features. There was strength in her character and it showed through. She had an outward serenity that reflected her former happiness.

Benjamin realized what a beautiful woman she really was. And then, miraculously, in this special setting, he was able to perceive and understand a great deal more. He realized how she had drawn him out of his life of solitude, and he discerned for the first time her remarkable patience during the last months. How she must have suffered! And yet how kind and patient she had remained.

Benjamin finished his coffee quietly. He didn't know quite what to do, but he knew that something was about to happen. Then he stood and walked slowly over to Elizabeth. Leaning down toward her, he kissed her long and tenderly. Elizabeth looked up with the loveliest smile he had ever seen. She raised her left hand toward him and rested it gently on his arm, but then she seemed to hesitate to do anything else. They were still, as if they were enveloped by some event beyond their control. Then, Benjamin, still not knowing what to do, kissed her again. Finally he said something quite simple:

"Let's go for a walk together this afternoon; it's a beautiful day, and we can go off somewhere and enjoy the sunshine together."

Elizabeth stood up slowly and took his hand; they walked together to the other end of the sunroom and looked out at the garden and the trees. Elizabeth could not quite grasp what was happening, but she knew that it was some-thing good. She leaned against him in a subtle initiative that reflected a new confidence in his responsiveness, but she remained puzzled. She had adored him from the day they first met, so it was difficult for her to understand that he had fallen in love with her only now.

THE CHARIOT

Searching through his earliest memories, he could not form a clear image of his very first ride in a carriage. And yet, as he tried to penetrate back to his infancy, the memory of such a ride was there, however indefinite. He was able to recall a vague sense of motion and an occasional small bump, and occasionally there was a feeling that he was being tilted - which all comprised those early baby carriage rides. Now, as he looked back, it seemed as if it must have been very pleasant to be pushed about, exercising no effort on his own part. But somehow, as the vague memory kept returning, all was not so pleasant. There was a helpless feeling, a feeling that he could not move at will out of a cramped position. Then too, a sense of nausea developed at times - whenever the carriage was rocked instead of pushed. And the hot sun with its glaring light was right in his eyes. When he cried the nearby talking continued, as if they took no heed of his discomfort.

But it was all so distant now. Did he actually remember that first baby carriage ride, or was he told about those days when he was carriage-bound? And was it a baby carriage or a stroller? It was not possible for him to know, and peering back, he saw only a murky darkness with shadows of past events. But he was quite sure of one thing, that there were ancient feelings that were true. Even now, whenever he rode in any vehicle which like the carriage had non-pneumatic tires, he would experience a feeling that was rooted deep within himself, a sensation that returned without form or rationale, but with a very familiar, and basic, inner consciousness.

His second memory of a carriage experience was sharper; it was cheerful and everything that a boy could want. It was a handsome carriage, and pulling it was a pony. The carriage was small so that a boy could climb in and no adults could fit in, and the pony would take him wherever he wanted. This was clearly not imagination, and he remembered precisely where he had actually ridden in such a carriage; it was when his parents took him to the park. And the sheer enchantment of it had stayed with him for many weeks! And even now as he thought back, he could see that carriage and pony. Once again, the clear and simple intensity of pleasure returned, unencumbered by all the tribulations of later years - the bad experiences that mar the purity of childhood joy. And he did recall that as he rode about there had been a certain smell, a smell of pony. Not that he minded it; his admiration of that creature with its long ears and fur, its flowing mane, as well as a dignified expression, was in no way reduced by that pungent reminder of reality. The young mind accepted what its senses received without question of desirability. However, the smell did bring the experience to earth, and the dreams of the experience, when they returned, were stronger but aesthetically mixed because of the pungent reminder. There had been at times a certain fear of the large animal. It seemed friendly enough, but it was big for him, and it was always unpredictable in its nervousness. None the less he loved him, and the whole thing was remembered as pleasure - and real it was. And even now he wished that he could experience it once again.

But the pleasant nature of such an experience is clearly not the existence of a carriage, but its availability at a time when a boy is still small and knows better than later in life how to indulge the sensuality of such simple pleasure fully. Even owning such a carriage now would not return the enjoyment. So it is the memory itself which is the precious thing. Now, the lost enjoyment regained, he could completely savor the fun of it without any of the fear that tinged it then. So, deeply now, the pure illusion rekindled the pleasure - timeless, and full, and forever fresh. And he knew now that these episodic pleasures are essential to a happy childhood, since much of a child's life is not as casually lived as it is remembered. The tears had come more often at that young age than they ever did later, and spankings had hurt more than any later pain. And he knew that this was so for everyone - more or less - but he knew also that not everyone remembers it for what it was.

Horses and carriages were to play a recurrent role in his life. And the next memory was of a crisper type, the kind that comes when consciousness is clarified by the acquired speech with which to describe it. It was racing horses which had become his way of life. So the next memory was of a racing sulky, and in front of it a magnificent horse. Jet black, head high, mane flowing, and tail erect, it had those powerfully developed muscles that are set to burst beneath the fur. Greater than all of that, however, was the haughty air, the overbearing posture, and the competitive expression that mark a horse which wants to win. And this, not because it is driven, but because it wants to win for its own sake. Dominance was so fully expressed in a horse such as this that it simply could not stand to see another of its kind pass ahead of it. And it was this that made a winner.

As he gazed at these images of times past, it was really himself at the reins that he saw the most. Full of strength and grace, and fuller yet of his own prowess, he drove all his horses hard. Throughout this time, the prime of his life, he and his beloved horses vied with each other to achieve supremacy, and they could not be beaten. And win they did, and win again, and yet again, they did. What a time it had been, this prime of life!

But it was not all enjoyment, for he could remember it now as a period of great exertion. There was no rest, no time to enjoy the things he had. And winning was an obsession, and fear of failure haunted him, and always there was so little time. Always, there were the racing schedules, the business transactions, the training and warm-ups, and the planning for strategies that win.

And as he now thought back to those times so long gone by, it was with mixed emotions. But if he could take those reins again, for even one hour, he would jump at the chance. Whatever else it was, or was not, it was fulfillment. And what a magnificent bunch of horses they had been to own!

Now things moved more slowly, and he could look back with contemplation. There was so much gone by since those heady days. And time was aplenty now. It filled the air around him, and he hardly knew any use for it. Searching, he gazed through that murky past for a clearer view of the horses and the carriages, but often even the memories failed him.

So now, he sat in that comfortable chair in his living room, looking out the picture window upon the lake below. With his eyes half closed, he slept a little, awakened, and slept again.

Suddenly, very distantly, he thought he could see something! Could it be a horse and carriage? But they were too distant and too small for certainty. His eyes remained riveted upon that distant image, and it appeared to be moving very fast toward him with dust rising on either side. So fast it moved, that before his very eyes the shape was becoming clearer. Soon he was completely sure of what it was.

The vehicle was a chariot. Yes, a chariot, very much like the ancient Roman chariots. And in front were three horses. How could it be moving so rapidly? For the first time there was a sense of fear. Initially, it was mostly uncertainty, that an ancient chariot should appear for no apparent or rational reason. Then too, it was moving so fast - faster than any vehicle he had ever seen. But the cold immobilizing fear that grew every moment was there because he understood full well that he had no control over this chariot.

There was no longer any way to measure the time that passed, except by the incredible speed and apparent growth of the chariot. Faster and faster it came - and shorter and shorter the time. Almost magically, it seemed upon him and filled most of the view throughout the light in front of him. To his consternation he could now see all the details.

The horses were magnificent and large. All three were jet black - with long flowing manes. Their hooves struck at the ground, and he could hear the rhythmic pounding of the soil. The muscles of their shoulders bulged as they strained violently. Foam was at their mouths. All their blackness was broken only by two spots. It was the white of their eyes that protruded on each side, with small broken veins from which streaks of blood flowed freely. The frenzy of their expression was fixed upon him. He knew now that he should turn and run away, as he would have in his youth. But now he was rooted to the spot, not able to move, not caring to struggle more. He knew, as if by some ancient message, that this immutable force was here for him - for him and for the rest of his kind, which could not take the simple measures to save themselves. And the fear became cold and moist, but he knew of no escape.

So he sat staring through the picture window of his living room, through that window that faced out on the lake below, and he stared at those wild horses, that vision of horror and excitement, coming straight toward him. And then it happened! The horses crashed through the glass, and the heavy chariot with thundering noise was over him. And just as suddenly, it was all finished. The noise had passed, all light was gone, and yes, even the fear was lifted from him. But it was not as if he lay there in tranquility to gaze at it all. Instead it was all nothing. No sight, no sound, no dust, and no moving shapes.

Still, out there beyond the broken glass, the waters of the lake below and the earth of the land were there without him. And they would go on for a time - a time as long as anyone's conception allowed. And yet one day, beyond all that foreseeable time, even the waters and the earth would go. Then, perhaps only gases would float about where this earth had all been, where so much seemed to have taken place. And, who knows, perhaps even the gases would float away.

ABOUT THE AUTHOR

Born of American parents abroad, Philip Edward Duffy lived in France, Poland, Czechoslovakia, and America. A graduate of Columbia College and Medical School, he interned at the Long Island Division of Kings County Hospital and served a residency at the Hospital of the University of Pennsylvania. As an Army reservist he was recalled to active service in the Far East, where he served as a medical officer during the Korean Conflict. Subsequently he became Professor of Neurology at the State University of New York in Syracuse, and later Professor of Neuropathology and Director of the Neuropathology Division at the Columbia University College of Physicians and Surgeons. He is the author of many medical and scientific articles, and a book on the astrocyte cells of the human brain; he was the Editor and contributor to a text and taped lecture series in neuropathology. Winner of the Joseph Mather Smith Prize, he was also for many years a member of the editorial board of the Journal of Neuropathology and Experimental Neurology.

From his life in Europe and America, through his medical career, and the varied experiences of military service in the Far East, Philip Duffy remained an interested observer of human nature. He expresses his observations in the fictional characters of his short stories, which he wrote over many years but brought to fruition as Professor Emeritus of Columbia University. If you find a part of yourself in these stories of the human experience, it is because the circumstances and emotions of life that they depict are universal.